DAMAGED DADDY BEAR

SHIFTERS OF THE AEGIS 1

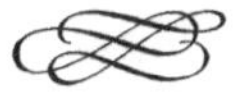

LEELA ASH

TABITHA ST. GEORGE

CONTENTS

*B*reakfast, as always, was a madhouse.

Rex Fairburn stood tall in the midst of the chaos, waving a spatula like a conductor's wand. "Micah, phone is turned off at the table. Nate, sit down. Sam, eat your eggs."

"They're *raw!*" the littlest boy whined.

"They're not raw. Eat. Micah? Phone, now."

At six foot four and 230 pounds, Rex could quiet a rioting bar just by walking in. One look at that square, hard face and tower of muscles silenced most men. And when he turned the laser focus of his piercing brown eyes on someone, the wildest of outlaw bikers suddenly developed manners.

That cold gaze now turned on Sam, who was prodding his egg yolks with a knife.

The four-year-old was not intimidated. "They jiggle! They're *raw!*" he howled in disgust.

"Samuel..."

Light as it was, the note of displeasure in his voice was like a grenade going off in the middle of the table. With a wail of infinite sadness, little Sam burst into tears. "They're *raaaaaw*! Don't make me eat raw!"

Three pairs of accusing eyes rolled up at him. Micah slipped his phone in his pocket, warned by the meltdown that, today, his father meant business. Nate, Sam's brother, froze and clutched his fork. The fear in the little boy's eyes drove a dagger through Rex's heart. Even his daughter, Eden, the one *good child* at the table this morning, looked up from breakfast and sighed.

Great. My eight-year-old daughter is disappointed in my parenting skills.

How many times had his wife, Ashley, given him that same look? When he couldn't bring himself to touch the baby's dirty diaper. That evening, he let the kids gorge themselves on cotton candy and they rampaged through the house all night long. No, Rex was *very* familiar with the look a man earned when he let down the lady of the house.

Which, these days, was little Eden. A fact that depressed him even further.

"Sam, Sam, c'mon. Calm down. It's okay."

"No! No! It's raw!"

What the hell was wrong with this kid? Who got this upset about an over-easy egg?

Eden knew, even if he didn't. "Dad? Last time Judy babysat us, she cooked Sam's eggs until they were all dry. That's how his mom made them for him."

And, in a heartbeat, the mystery was solved. Four months ago, Rex's best friends, Adam and Maria Long, were murdered. Shot when they stopped to help a guy broken down on the side of the road. A man who turned out to be a drug dealer on the run. In their will, they left custody of their two sons, Nathanial and Samuel, to him.

That still surprised him. Entrusting your kids to a single dad with two children of his own.

Adam and Maria must have had a higher opinion of me than I do.

This morning's hysteria wasn't about eggs. It was about two little boys who'd had their lives ripped apart. And about a man who knew what that felt like—and shouldn't expect them to 'get over it' in a few short months.

With a quick smile to Eden, Rex peered down at Sam's plate. "Huh. Heck, they *are* jiggling, aren't they? I think you're right. I think they *are* raw."

That dialed the tear faucet back to a slow trickle. Sam sniffed and poked the egg. "They shouldn't move."

"Gotcha. Well, that's easy to fix." Rex scooped the plate up and headed back to the stove. "Two well-done eggs, coming right up."

As he slid the offending food back onto the skillet, the kids relaxed and returned to breakfast. Nate selected a piece of toast and began to delicately nibble out its middle.

Dammit. I forgot he hates crusts. I was supposed to cut those off.

Ashley would have remembered. Same for Maria. But neither woman was here anymore. Just him. The sole survivor of two families.

Eh, screw that pity-party. You're not the sole survivor. Four little kids pulled through too.

Kids who needed him. To protect them and love them. To raise them up to be fine adults. And, yes, to fry their eggs until they were rock hard, if that's what it took.

"Two eggs, *not* raw!" Rex flipped the rubbery monstrosities back onto Sam's plate and was rewarded with a teary smile.

For three minutes—three *whole* minutes—peace reigned over the table. Kids chomped eggs and bacon, slurped their cereal. Phones disappeared. Boys sat still... or still-ish. Rex savored that brief moment of sanity and sipped his coffee.

Micah, the oldest, at ten, finally broke the quiet. "Dad, can we go to Totten Reservoir today?"

"You'll have to ask Judy." The sitter still hadn't answered the message he left her, but she was reliable.

Or, reliable-ish. "Ish" seemed to be the operative word of the day.

Four small faces turned up to him, dark with frowns. "Why can't you take us?" Eden protested.

"There's an important meeting this afternoon. I have to go to it."

The boys simply looked glum. His daughter, however, planted her hands on her hips and went into full attack mode. "Dad!" Somehow, she turned that tiny word into a three-syllable howl of outrage. "That's not the deal! The deal is, you work all week as much as you have to, but weekends are for *us.*"

"Eden, this is a special event. It's...."

"Weekends are for *family.*"

Look at her. Despite her rebellion, Rex had to smile. The spitting image of her mother. He and Ashley were Bear Shifters, and nothing mattered more to a Bear than family. Eden might only be eight, but she was the daughter of her parents. A tiny little Cub, a Momma Bear to be, who wasn't going to let anyone–not even her own father–mess with her home.

And she did have a point. A developer and self-made millionaire, Rex put in long hours at work. Terrible hours. Though it killed him to admit it, that scatterbrain Judy spent more time with his kids than he did.

I have to do that. I need to provide for them. That work puts a roof over their heads, feeds and clothes them. Someday, it will send them to college–something my parents never did for me.

All true. But it didn't change the fact that he was gone all day, every day of the work week.

Or the fact that he'd promised to keep his weekends free.

"How about this, Eden? I'll take Monday off from work. That way we'll still have a weekend."

"It's not when weekends are supposed to be, though."

When did his kids get so finicky? "True. But it means I'll only work four days before the next weekend."

That was the key. Eden nodded, satisfied that this was a good trade.

"As an added bonus, how about if we head to the mall on Sunday and–"

The chime of his doorbell interrupted his offer. Who came calling at 8:30 am on a Saturday morning? Rex scowled–then almost laughed when Eden's face lit up with outrage too. Nobody else had better mess with *her* weekend!

You watch. It'll be Judy. I asked her to sit from 1:00 to 8:00. Instead, she'll show up at 8:30 in the morning, 'late', and plan to leave at noon.

Damn, he needed to find another sitter.

But when he opened the door, it wasn't to find Judy's friendly (if vacant) face.

A man in dusty leathers stood on his doorstep. Aaron King, the Alpha of the local Wolf Pack. Lean, weathered, and rangy, King wore his hair long and pulled back in a ponytail. Streaks of grey threaded through his hair and handlebar mustache. From long experience, though, Rex knew that age hadn't dulled the edge of his fierce strength and independence.

"Mr. King. How can I help you?"

"I'd like a word about this meeting you called."

Pretty much what he'd expected. "Of course. Come on in."

Neither man offered any small talk as they strode back down the hall. Passing the kitchen, Rex paused. "Kids, I'll be right back. I need to talk to Mr. King for a minute."

Thankfully, the arrival of a 'stranger' put them all on their best behavior. "Hi, Mr. King!" Eden chirped.

"Good morning, Miss Fairburn."

Rex waved at the two smallest boys. "I don't believe you've met these guys. They're Nathanial and Samuel Long."

"Adam and Maria's boys?" When he nodded, the Wolf grimaced. "I was sorry to hear about your parents. They were good people."

"Sam, Nate, this is Mr. King. He's the Alpha of the Sand Pack."

King shot him a sideways glance. "You don't hide Shifter business from them?"

"Nope." Rex met his gaze firmly, but there was no challenge in the Wolf's face. "They're all Bears, or Bear Kin, and I want them to know it. I won't risk having one of my kids become Lost."

He almost added, '...if I die.' Given what the Long boys had been through, though, that didn't need to be said out loud.

"Good. Nothing more messed up than a Shifter who doesn't know what he is."

Yeah, that was a hell of a thought. Lose touch with the Shifter community and you grow up thinking you are nothing more than a plain, normal human... until your first Shift. He wouldn't wish that on anybody. If his kids got orphaned, it damn well wouldn't happen to them.

"We'll be down in the office if you guys need us. Micah, Eden? Make sure everyone's plates get in the sink, hear me?"

"Yes, Dad," they said in unison.

"Thank you." Nodding to the Wolf, he gestured down the hall. "This way."

When people thought of Colorado, they imagined towering tree-clad mountains. Here in the southwestern part of the state, the land was dry and flat. The picture windows of Rex's study offered wide, sweeping views of... well, a whole lot of nothing.

Still, he liked the desert with its scruffy, stubborn resilience. So did King. The Wolf eyed the scrub and stone, drinking in the sight of the wilderness.

As soon as the door clicked shut, King cut straight to the point. "Why did you ask the Dragons of the First Flight to come here?"

"Mesa Verde National Park has seen twenty-four cases of vandalism over the last–"

King cut him short with a chop of his hand. "I can read the news. We've got a rash of teenage jackasses this summer. So what?"

"I think it's more than that."

"Pot thieves? Sure, happens all the time. But why involve outsiders? Even if this turns out to be Shifter business, no one knows this place better than the people who live here."

"Who I've also invited to this meeting," Rex countered. No damned Wolf was going to challenge him!

"But why the outsiders?"

"I think there's something going on, something bigger than greedy treasure hunters. And I think the First Flight might know something about it."

"Why?" the Wolf sneered. "Not one of them has ever set foot in this land."

"No, but they have a Wellspring. A living one."

"Really? You believe the First Flight has a magical fountain? A gateway to the Other Side?" His lip curled back even farther. "Aren't you a bit old to believe in fairy tales?"

Anger set Rex's brown eyes alight and he straightened to his full height, glaring down at the smaller man. "You come into my home and insult me?"

Wolves backed down before few things. Yet, only a fool

confronted a Bear in his den. "I chose my words poorly," King admitted.

Not a full apology, but Rex relented. "You did. I have a cousin from Ohio who says he's seen this Wellspring. I won't have him called a liar."

"Hmm." The Wolf wasn't persuaded—but he wasn't brazen enough to push the issue. "There'll be problems, you know."

"I expect so."

"The Dragons of the Snow Flight won't come."

"I invited them. If they choose not to come, that's their business."

"I won't go," King added.

Now that did surprise him. "Why?"

"There are debts of blood and honor between my Pack and the Snow Flight. I will not break bread with their enemies."

"Are they truly enemies?" *That* was something he didn't need: two warring Flights of Dragons!

"There's bad blood between them."

"Do you know what caused it?"

King shook his head. "No. Not my Pack, not my problem." Without another word, he headed toward the door.

"That's all you wanted to know?"

"Yup," the Wolf said. "You're not a Wolf, but you're sensible. Couldn't figure out why you'd drag outsiders into our business."

His eyes raked over the Bear once, hard and cool. "Still not sure it's a good decision."

"I guess we'll find out this afternoon."

CHAPTER 2

Twenty festive paper plates. Twenty birthday hats. Twenty sets of party favors, ready for fun.

And one small, very sad boy.

With a sinking heart, Paige Hall gazed around the room she'd rented at Play Time Pizza. Crepe paper streamers bounded about the ceilings. From every wall, posters of cartoon characters yelled, "Happy Birthday, Jake!" A lovely chocolate cake, eight candles circling its edge, waited in the kitchen.

Only one thing was missing.

Guests.

"Mommy? What time is it?"

Late. More than a half hour after this 'party' was supposed to begin. But how could she tell Jake that?

This was supposed to be *his* day. In April, they'd arrived in Cortez, Colorado. Two months was nowhere near enough time for a boy to make friends–especially not a shy child, like Jake. Paige thought she'd come up with a fix for that. Cake, presents, pinball machines, and a ball pit to bribe classmates to come to his birthday party. Twenty phone calls to twenty sets of parents. Twenty assurances that yes, of course, Little Johnny and Susie would be delighted to come.

Now, on the Big Day....

Nothing. Not one child or parent. No calls to cancel. Not even a text or an email to warn her that her dreams for her son were collapsing, silently.

"It's... late, honey." She stroked his hair, hoping to take some of the sting out of those words.

Jake wasn't comforted. A tiny ball of misery, he stared bleakly at the cheerful decorations. Tears rose in his eyes. "Nobody's coming, are they?"

"Well, we're coming, right?"

Lame. Horribly lame, even to her ears. Her son hung his head. "Why do people hate me?"

"Jake, no." Paige dropped to her knees and swept him into a hug. "Nobody hates you. They just don't know you yet. You'll make friends in the fall when school starts again."

Most kids would bawl. Jake just sat there, stiff and silent, tears streaming down his cheeks.

The waitress caught her eye and held up the cake. Paige shook her head and mouthed, 'Box.'

"You know, it's the first week of summer. I bet a lot of kids are going to camp or they're on vacation." If so, their parents could have mentioned that–instead of pretending they'd show up. That was an issue for another day, however. Right now, she just wanted to salvage at least a tiny shred of happiness for her boy.

"Why did we have to come here?"

Because Los Angeles was too expensive and dangerous. Because cockroaches scurried about their nasty apartment, the only thing she could afford. Because she'd been mugged walking home from work one night. Because drug dealers lurked around the one rusty playground in their 'neighborhood.'

And because of Leonard. Because his drinking had spiraled out of control... *again*... and she suspected that, this time, meth was fueling the chaos. Nine years she'd given him. Time to clean himself up. To do right by her and marry her. To become the father... the *man* that her son needed.

Well, she was done with waiting. The night he came home covered with another woman's lipstick was the breaking point. They'd left the next morning, all of their worldly belongings packed in two suitcases, while Leonard snored away on the couch surrounded by empty bottles.

"Mommy had her reasons." Adult reasons, ones a child wouldn't understand. "But it will work out. I promise. It's just going to take some time."

The waitress slunk over and quietly set the boxed cake on their table. Paige slipped her a credit card. Play Time wasn't going to refund her money just because no guests arrived.

Another bill I can't afford. And all I did was hurt him.

"Tell you what. Why don't you and I do something special? Just the two of us. We can...."

The notes of her ring tone interrupted. The happy little song stirred something dark and furious in Paige's heart.

If that's some deadbeat mom, telling me—45 minutes late!—that they won't make it, I will lose my shit. Completely.

"Hello?" Voice neutral, she steeled herself.

"Heya Paige!"

Judy Darling. Her neighbor, not some delinquent parent. Relief washed over her, though it was frosted by disappointment. Some furious, hard part of her soul really *wanted* to chew someone's head off right now.

"Hi, Judy. What's up?"

"I'm in Denver!"

"Nice." Paige gritted her teeth and waited for the shoe to fall. When they first arrived, Judy was a bundle of joy and welcome. A promise from heaven that things would be different here in Colorado. Friendlier. Kinder. Safer. Yet, as the weeks rolled by, she noticed that if her neighbor stopped by to visit, it usually meant she needed something.

Eh, that was unfair. Judy watched Jake every day while Paige worked. Sure, her neighbor expected to be paid, and the cost of sitting took a huge chunk out of her paycheck. But the rate was far lower than what she charged her other clients. For cutting a single mom a deal, Judy earned a right to the occasional favor.

Unaware of her inner debate, her neighbor prattled on. "I know, right? Dave and I are having a *blast!*"

"Dave?"

"This really cool guy I met at a party last night."

So, you met last night... and now you're in Denver with him.

Okay, she was *not* touching that with a ten foot stick. God knows, her own taste in men wasn't perfect. But that was just foolish.

"Anyway, I was wondering if there was something you could help me with."

Of course. Paige sighed. "What's up? It's not a good time. It's Jake's birthday."

"Oh, hey! Wish the little dude Happy Birthday for me!"

"Sure." She waited, but Judy seemed to have forgotten why she called. "What do you need help with?"

"Oh, right! I totally spaced. I was supposed to babysit today, and I totally forgot."

And now Judy was in Denver, on the other side of the state. That *was* a significant problem–for somebody else.

"I'd love to Judy, but like I said, it's Jake's birthday and...."

"It's only for five hours. And it pays thirty bucks an hour."

A hundred and fifty dollars? For five hours of sitting? Paige's jaw dropped. Hell, that would just about cover the cost of this horrible 'party.'

"That's... amazing. But I don't have anyone to watch Jake and–"

"Take the little dude along! Rex has four kids of his own. Nobody'll notice one more."

That might work... and she could really, *really* use the money....

"Okay. Sure."

"Thank you! You are a life saver!" Judy crowed. "It's Rex Fairburn. 125 Dry Gulch Road."

That name set off alarms in her head. "Hang on. This isn't the Rex Fairburn that owns Ancient Ways, is it?"

"Yep. That, and about six more resorts. Plus a couple of ski lodges too."

Paige gulped. "He's my boss."

"Oh, cool! So you know him already!"

"Uh, no. Not really." Owners didn't fraternize with housecleaning staff like her. She'd never even seen the man.

"Oh, that's okay. He's totally cool. You'll love him."

'Cool'? Judy, Paige decided, seriously needed a few more words in her vocabulary. "When do I need to be there?"

"Eleven thirty."

"Tonight?"

Her neighbor giggled. "No, silly. 11:30 am."

"Judy!" she wailed. "That was fifteen minutes ago!"

"Was it? Oh, wow."

'Oh, wow'? That was all she could say? "I'm already late!"

"I told you I spaced." A sulky note crept into Judy's voice.

Dammit, this was the last thing she needed!

A sick feeling swept over her as she glanced about the festive, empty, room.

No, the last thing I need is to not be able to buy groceries next week because I blew all my money on this failure of a party. My supervisor turned down my last request for an advance on my paycheck.

"Fine. I'll do it."

"Thanks so much, Paige! I knew I could count on you! And say hi to the little dude for me!"

With that, she hung up.

Jake watched her, glum and hopeless.

"Judy says Happy birthday."

"Is she coming to my party?"

"No, she can't. She's in Denver." The last tiny spark of hope died from his eyes. "Look, baby. We need to do a favor for Judy. We have to spend the afternoon at someone's house. Is that okay?"

"I guess." Jake slipped his party hat off and set it down carefully beside his clean plate.

What a horrible birthday. A no-guest 'party' and then work with your mom. Guilt and shame set Paige's stomach roiling.

This day was going to be a horror story from beginning to end.

CHAPTER 3

*H*er first glimpse of 125 Dry Gulch Road nearly sent Paige fleeing for the hills.

Stone walls, six feet tall, lined the road. After passing through its great wrought-iron gate, the driveway curved a quarter of a mile back to the house. Admittedly, the land was scrub and brush, not manicured lawns. But still, that was a huge tract of land for one man to own! Plus, the house at the end of that drive was anything but normal. Two stories tall, it swept along the crest of a small rise. One entire wall of the house was glass, giving every room a sweeping, panoramic view of the desert. A lake-sized pool lounged off to the side, complete with sauna, slides, and an Olympic diving board.

Well, Mr. Fairburn is a developer. Of course, he's got a nice house.

Jake gaped at that sky-high diving board. "Can I go swimming?"

"We'll see, honey."

Four cars sat in the detached garage. A black Ford Expedition, a Humvee, a battered Jeep and some sleek sporty car Paige didn't recognize.

15

That was a *lot* of cars for one person!

Carefully, she pulled up in front of the mansion. "Jake, could you wait here for a minute? I want to make sure I've got the right place."

Not true. But if Mr. Fairburn lost his cool over her tardiness, Jake didn't need to hear it. Not today.

Under the hot June sun, the tar of the drive burned straight through her cheap sandals. Paige clutched her purse like a safety blanket and hurried across to the shadowy arch of the front door.

As soon as she pressed the doorbell, heavy footsteps thundered down the hall. She had one moment to think, *Oh, that does not sound good...* Then the door was yanked open, violently.

The man within towered over her like an enraged grizzly. Broad shouldered, tall, he was the largest man she'd ever seen. Stretched to its limits, an 'Ancient Ways' t-shirt struggled to cover his barrel chest and muscular arms. Despite his size, there wasn't an ounce of fat on his enormous form.

And he wasn't happy. On a better day, he could be the poster boy for the Southwest. Weathered, craggy features, hardened by the desert. Rich brown eyes to soften the harshness of his features.

Eyes that, today, blazed with fury.

"This is a *miserable* time to be late, Miss..."

For one second, that scowl wavered. "Hang on. You're not Judy Darling."

"No, I'm her neighbor Paige Hall. Judy couldn't make it today and asked if I'd cover for her." She held her hand out.

He didn't take it. "Where is she?"

"She... got called out of town last night?" Heavens, here she was, lying to her employer to save the neck of her useless neighbor.

"And what made her think that I would entrust my children," he spat, "to some woman I've never met?"

Under his furious gaze, Paige's heart hammered. She forced herself not to lick her lips. "Actually, sir, I work for you. I'm one of the house cleaning staff at Ancient Ways."

"Sadly, that's not much of a recommendation," he snorted. "My head of house-keeping is an idiot. She can't do a background check to save her life. She's hired three felons and a swarm of petty criminals."

Well, that was one thing they agreed on: Mrs. Gordon had her head up her ass. But that didn't seem like a good conversational gambit to Paige.

"And I can see that Miss Darling recommended someone as tardy and thoughtless as herself."

Okay, there was a limit to the abuse she'd take for $150 bucks! "For your information, *sir*, Judy called me fifteen minutes ago. I got here as fast as I could. If you don't want me, just say the word and I'm gone."

A glance at his watch set the big man seething. "Dammit, I am already late!" Still, he hesitated, scowling at her, until a movement drew his eye to her car. "Did you bring your child with you?"

"Yes. Jake. I didn't have anyone to watch him and Judy said this was an emergency." Maybe that would push him over the edge. At this point, Paige just wanted to go home.

Instead, his frown softened. "Most criminals don't bring their children along, I admit."

How 'generous' of him. She waited, stewing, until he sighed.

"Fine. You can't be worse than Miss Darling."

One hundred and fifty dollars, Paige reminded herself as she gritted her teeth. *I need this.*

"I have a very important meeting, for which I am *already*

late. I should be home before dinner. Micah!" he bawled. The unexpected shout made her jump.

At the end of the hall, a gangly boy stuck his head around the corner and scowled at his furious father. "Yeah?"

"This is your new babysitter for today. You're in charge of introductions. I have to go."

"Sure. Whatever." The boy gave her a speculative look. One that didn't bode well to Paige.

Let me guess. Once poppa's out the door, he's going to tell me that normally, they have ice cream for lunch. And oh, Judy always lets them play video games all day long.

Well, she'd deal with that. Kids would be kids. Paige waved her son over.

He scrambled out, eyeing Rex nervously. "Mommy? Should I bring the cake?"

"Um...."

For the first time, her employer noticed the balloons in the back seat. "You dragged your son out of his own birthday party for this job?" His face lit with outrage.

That look, that disdain, was the last straw. "Listen, *you!*" Paige hissed, poking him in the chest with a stiff finger. "I just threw a birthday party that nobody came to. Now, I get that this meeting is important to you. But my son is having one of the worst days in his life. If you do anything–one single little thing!–to make him feel worse, I am out of here. Screw you and your stupid job!"

Too late, she remembered who she was talking to. Rex Fairburn didn't control just this babysitting job–he owned the resort where she cleaned. One word from him and her world collapsed.

At that moment, she didn't care. Her life, this town, these people... they all sucked. She'd be damned if she'd let Jake suffer for her miserable choices.

To her shock, her furious defense didn't drive him into a

frenzy. Instead, he suddenly seemed to truly see her. To realize that a human being, not a misbehaving robot, stood before him. "Of course," he muttered, his voice dropping to a bass growl. "I would not wish to upset the child."

The pause that followed was awkward, though a relief. "Can your children have birthday cake? I don't want to take leftovers home. I want Jake to forget this day as quickly as possible."

"Yes. Of course."

"Thank you." Turning to her son, she forced herself to smile and call out, "Sure, bring it, sweetie!"

Another glance at his watch, and Rex winced. "Forgive me. I *have* to go."

"Okay." As soon as she stepped out of his way, he hustled for the Jeep. Strange choice for an important meeting! "Um, any dietary restrictions? Rules?"

"No. Well, there are rules, but I don't have time. Just don't let them do anything crazy!"

Jake sidled up to her as the Jeep tore away.

Four children watched her now. All fairly young, she was pleased to see. Jake might have a good time after all. "Hi! I'm Paige. Judy couldn't make it today and she asked me to sit for her."

"I'm Micah," said the oldest boy. "This is my sister, Eden. And these are Nate and Sam."

How odd. Why didn't he call them his brothers? Also, little Sam looked as nervous as her own son. "Nice to meet you. This is my son, Jake."

'Hi' got muttered several times.

"So...," Micah began.

Here comes the request for the ice cream lunch.

"Do you like Totten Reservoir? Because we go there a lot. With Judy."

Okay, that was a reasonable request. Though Paige had a

better suggestion. "Totten?" she let her nose wrinkle. "It's okay. Pretty crowded on weekends, though. Have you ever heard of Sweetwater Creek?"

Micah shook his head.

"You have to walk to get to it, but there's never anyone there. It has rocks you can slide down and a little pool at the bottom for swimming. Plus, the best part is that there are some old ruins right there."

She had them at 'sliding down rocks'. Four little jaws dropped.

"If you want, I can pack us a picnic lunch. We can eat beside the creek and spend the afternoon swimming and exploring."

"Cool!" Micah breathed. Delight lit the faces of all his siblings.

Even Jake smiled and Paige felt the first knot around her heart unravel.

Maybe something could be salvaged from this terrible day after all!

CHAPTER 4

Of course, today was the day when everyone arrived promptly.

Except Rex.

By the time he jogged into the Hohokam Conference Room at Ancient Ways, an hour late, he expected to find the room empty. Maybe with some obscene graffiti spray-painted on the walls by a Pack of Wolves pissed off about driving twelve hours for a no-show Bear.

Instead, he found the room filled to the brim with the Shifters of the Four Corners area. Grumpy, surly... but still here. The buffet table was demolished; staff bustled in and out, refilling the trays and beer coolers. Looked like the only 'revenge' he'd earned was people trying to eat him out of hearth and home.

Well, let 'em. Plenty more where that came from.

Quickly, he surveyed the crowd. A couple dozen Bears from all across the southwest. Representatives of six different Wolf Packs. They handled the delay worst, pacing about the room like it was a zoo cage. In their midst stood a surprise: Lilianna King, daughter of Aaron King.

Nice to know King's kid doesn't obey any better than my little ones.

"Fairburn. Finally decided to show up, huh?" Brown hair cropped in a shaggy bob cut framed a delicate, Elvin face. Between that face and her pretty name, many men treated her like a fragile flower.

Once. Then she taught them how wrong they were.

Rex never made that mistake. He'd seen her pound mortal men into the ground in the cage fights out behind Scrub's Bar.

"Sorry, Lily." He gestured at the bottles scattered around her table. "Though at least it looks like my people didn't let you die of thirst."

Drunk Wolf Princesses. Greaaat. Just what every community gathering needs!

Over in the corner, a handful of desert Rats huddled together. Bulging backpacks surrounded them. Either they'd come prepared to camp for a month—or they were pilfering as much food and drink as they could carry. Rex's money was on the latter, though he didn't mind. The woman in their center, a wizened old hag who looked like the world's skee-viest grandmother, was SueSue Mint. She'd tipped him off to the extent of his 'problem.' So, if the Rat wanted a week's groceries as a reward, she could have them.

A score of Witch Hares had commandeered the window tables. Most were loners, women who kept to themselves and worked old, traditional magic. Rex also spotted six Hares from the Sedona Warren, the region's most prestigious coven. Good. If anyone could solve his problem, it would probably be one of those women.

But where was the guest of honor? There was supposed to be a Dragon here....

Looking closer, he spotted *two*, not one.

A shadowy stranger sat in the corner, watching the crowd

with a steely, disapproving gaze. Black suit, black hair, and brown eyes so dark they almost seemed to match his funereal clothes. Rex started toward him–then hesitated. One Shifter could often catch a glimpse of another's animal soul. This guy was a Dragon. Yet two slender horns crowned the head of his Dragon, curving down along its neck.

Snow Flight. Those were the only Dragons with that distinctive crest.

I guess Aaron King wasn't right about anything!

Rex didn't recognize this guy. The Flight laired in the Sierra Nevada's and he rarely had cause to travel up there. King's Sand Pack had ancient ties to the Flight. Other than that, the Dragons didn't have much use for other Shifters.

So, where was the guy from the First Flight?

There. Over by the buffet. Waiting patiently for the cocktail wieners to be refilled.

From his first glance, Rex was impressed. Few men were his equal in size. This Dragon was one of them. A hulking square-jawed brute with short blonde hair. Even his Dragon looked like a bruiser. Scars crisscrossed its white scales, and several were missing good-sized chunks. This was a warrior, one who'd seen years of battle.

And one who isn't *a cultured sophisticate. No chance that the Wolves will take him for a dandy and decide he needs to be taken down a few pegs.*

Good choice on the First Flight's part. Nobody was starting shit with this guy.

Stepping around the table, Rex offered his hand. "Rex Fairburn. You must be from the First Flight."

"Yup. Finn Donnelly." No blame or irritation colored his voice, and his grip was firm. "Everything okay? I worried this trip might start with a rescue mission."

"I hate to admit this, but…" Rex dropped his voice. "…it was babysitter problems."

The Dragon snorted. "Some days, life just won't give you a break."

"Tell me about it. Shall we get started? I'll do the presentation on the situation, then pass the mike to you."

"Bree's the one you want for that." Finn pointed at a leggy Hare, chattering away in the middle of the other Witches.

A mane of flame-red hair, a shoulder-less white blouse, and a split dress that flaunted those legs. "The Flight sent a Hare? Why?"

"Because she's smart. And, well, not a dick." The Dragon's voice dropped to a murmur. "That's kind of a rare commodity in my Flight."

Not just his Flight, either. Dragons had a rep for sailing in and assuming they were in charge. Because, well, they were *Dragons*. "So, who're you?"

"I'm her husband."

Oops. Eyes up, buddy.

Rex dragged his gaze away from those enchanting legs and up to a more respectful level. "And what do you do?"

Finn grinned, oblivious to how the Bear had ogled his wife. "I'm a good husband. I do what I'm told."

"Heh. Been there," he admitted.

All right. Showtime. Rex stepped up to the podium and prepared to eat crow.

"Hey folks. Sorry about the delay. Helluva thing to ask you to drive so far and then not show up on time. I am truly, deeply sorry for that."

The crowd quieted. Even the Wolves retreated to their tables, nursing beers. A room full of cautious, faintly hostile eyes rested upon the big man.

"I won't waste any more of your time. The reason I asked you to come is that I think there's something strange going on in the Four Corners area. Maybe something dangerous, to all of us."

He'd hoped that such a dramatic claim would win him the crowd's full attention. Instead, a couple of snorts and chuckles rang out across the room.

Not the reaction he'd wanted. Rex cleared his throat and continued. "Over the last two months, there have been twenty-four documented cases of vandalism near Mesa Verde National Park. Canyon of Ancients National Monument has had at least that many. Somebody is digging up old Puebloan ruins and—"

One of the Wolves howled with laughter. "Who gives a shit about stolen pots? It's probably the damned Rats."

SueSue hugged her backpack close but didn't jump to her Kind's defense.

"It's not Rats, and it's not pot-hunters," Rex growled, trying to stare the Wolf quiet. Bad move. The guy met his gaze, bristling, and his glower deepened. "A lot of these sites have been vandalized. There are runes, drawings, spray painted on the walls. Like someone's performing rituals."

"Teenagers," the Wolf scoffed. "You're afraid of punk kids."

Rex felt his temper begin to bubble up. "The hell I am. There's more. People have seen lights at these places—"

"Oooh, scary! Because no one's ever partied where they shouldn't."

A vein in the Bear's head began to throb. "—and there have been strange Shifters in this area. People no one knows, who don't talk to any of us."

That, at least, was a credible threat. "Who saw these Shifters?" a Bear asked.

Rex waved at the Rats. "SueSue and her Kin."

Once more, the Wolf burst out laughing. "Rats are lying, thieving shits. Why should we listen to anything they say? I bet they're making up stories to hide the fact that *they're* the ones stealing all those pots."

The mood in the room was shifting, and not in a good way. People murmured among themselves, a dull hum of annoyance. Bears checked their watches, Wolves snorted.

He was losing them. Losing his only hope to find out what was going on and fix it. Rex drew his breath, preparing to roar them back into submission.

Before he could, that red-headed Hare stood up. "Mr. Fairburn? I have an odd question. These ruins that have been vandalized—are they all circular buildings?"

The Bear's jaw snapped shut. "Uh, I don't know. Let me check."

The room quieted as he flipped through the folder of pictures he'd brought. For a moment, at least, the newcomer had recaptured people's attention.

"Yeah, they are. All of them. Hell, I hadn't even noticed that."

Now the Hares all leaned forward, curiosity piqued. "Are there small holes in these circular ruins?" Bree continued.

"Hmm..." Flip, flip, flip, went the pages. "Sorry, can't tell. The pictures don't show much. I can see a couple of holes, yeah, but..."

"What the hell is this all about?" the irate Wolf snarled.

Bree Donnelly fixed her unnerving, witchy gaze upon him. "Magic. Your 'partying teenagers' are targeting one very specific type of magical site. And, if I'm right, only locations that contain powerful artifacts."

Silence fell. She had their complete attention.

"Mr. Fairburn, could I take the podium?"

"Sure!" Rex retreated, delighted to hand the reins over. He drifted to the buffet table where Donnelly lounged, savoring a new plate of appetizers. "Damn, she'd good," he muttered to the Dragon.

"She certainly is." Donnelly beamed at his Mate.

Calm and at home in front of a crowd, Bree began to speak. Confirming every one of Rex's dark suspicions.

"All of these 'acts of vandalism' are taking place in kivas, the ceremonial buildings of the Puebloans. Modern kivas are square–but the oldest are round, which is why we know they're targeting the most ancient sites. And those holes? They're called '*sipapus*.' Supposedly, they're the gate where the first humans entered this world."

"Sound familiar?" Bree scanned the silent, attentive room. "We call them something different."

"Wellsprings," one of the Sedona Hares called out.

Wellsprings. Rex nodded. Just like his cousin from Ohio said.

Every Shifter child knew about them. Once upon a time (or so the stories went), doorways linked this world and the spirit realm, the Other Side. Wellsprings, they were called. Mystical pools that allowed magic and Shifter Spirit Animals to enter this world.

"Exactly." Bree nodded. "We believe that *sipapus* may be another form of Wellsprings, ones unique to the southwest."

Only Princess Lily remained immune to the spell the Hare wove. "So what? The Wellsprings died centuries ago. Why would anyone care about them?"

"They weren't dead," Bree replied. "They were dormant. And now, they're waking up."

Around them, the room filled with whispers and fidgeting. Rex took a sip of his beer. That was a hell of a bombshell to drop. Better her than him!

It certainly wasn't a claim that would go unchallenged. "Bullshit!" Lily glowered at the Witch.

Yet, Bree hadn't come here without proof and allies. The head of the Sedona Hares rose to her feet. "She's telling the truth. I know a couple of Warrens who've been studying the Wellsprings, trying to figure out what changed. In fact, if you weren't all magically blind, the proof is standing right in front of you." She waved a finger between Bree and Finn. "Anyone with the Gift can see power flowing between them. These two are Mates. True Mates, like in the old stories. They've gone through the Rite of Claiming–something you can't do without a living Wellspring."

The Rite of Claiming? Now, Rex found *himself* starting to wonder. Hell, that was even crazier than Wellsprings! Sure, in myth, Dragons recognized their soulmates and joined their spirits forever in a ritual called 'the Rite of Claiming.' But that didn't really happen.

Did it? He glanced over at Finn. Intent on his new plate of cocktail wieners, the big Dragon seemed unaware of the hullabaloo around him.

The Dragon from the Snow Flight wasn't, though. Tall Dark and Mysterious sat bolt upright, wide-eyed. Looking like he'd just been electrocuted.

Bet somebody's damn glad his Flight sent him here!

Fully in control of her audience once more, Bree kept the ball rolling. "She's right. Every Dragon in the First Flight has Claimed a Mate. Over the last three years, Wellsprings all around the world came to life once more."

Three years? That was a long time to keep a secret that would transform Shifter society!

Rex wasn't the only one to notice. Eyes narrowed, Lily glared at both Hares. "So, why are we only hearing about this now?"

"Because of the Fangs of Apophis. The people who may well be trying to kill all of you at this very moment."

Staring at the rapt faces around him, Rex felt laughter bubbling up from deep within himself.

Damn, Bree Donnelly knows how to work a crowd! Me, I would have lost my cool and punched that Wolf, and the whole room would have dissolved into one huge bar brawl.

"We have enemies," Bree declared. "Deadly ones. With bribery and blackmail, they lure Shifters to a life of crime. They kidnap Kin and threaten to murder them unless decent Shifters help them."

He half expected Lily to challenge that dramatic assertion, but the Wolf's brows narrowed in concentration and a strange uncertainty clouded her delicate features. "Who are these people and what do they want?"

"They call themselves 'the Fangs of Apophis'. Named after an evil god of ancient Egypt. They're led by Worms—Fallen Dragons who've chewed their wings off. A lot of Wolves joined them, some Hares and Bears. But the Rats have suffered the most. The Fangs routinely kidnap Rat Kin and use them as hostages. Because of that, they have a fantastic spy network."

SueSue shuffled to her feet and jerked a thumb at the Rats clustered around her. "We got Kin in southern California we can't find. You think the Fangs took them?"

"They may have, yes. Give me their names after we're done, and I'll pass them on to one of the Flight. We've managed to rescue almost 500 Kin so far."

Five *hundred*. Rex's head spun at that number. And those were only the ones rescued.

"What do the Fangs want?" Lily asked.

"Power. Money, riches... enough wealth to control governments. Plus, magic. They're trying to find the Wellsprings and turn them into weapons. They've also spent years accumulating magical antiquities. Things that sat in museums for centuries, dormant, like the Wellsprings. Now that magic is returning to the world, those talismans are coming alive too. And they're dangerous. One of them took out half a Flight of Dragons."

Gasps of shock echoed through the room. Rex glanced at

Donnelly and the scarred Dragon nodded. "Got me too," he confessed.

Hell, Dragons are as mean as Shifters get. If these Fangs can take out a bunch of them, what chance do I stand?

But as quickly as that self-doubt arose, his Bear spirit rebelled against it. A burning anger fanned to life, sending hot strength pouring through him. This was *his* town. *His* family lived here. There was no threat, no danger, a Bear wouldn't face to protect what he loved. Didn't matter who these Fangs were. They were in trouble if they messed with him.

"I know this must be a shock to all of you," Bree said, "but when Mr. Fairburn contacted us, it all sounded too suspicious. Strange Shifters lurking around the edges of your community. Weird rituals taking place in old, abandoned, magical sites. All revolving around something that sounds a heck of a lot like new Wellsprings."

The slim red-head threw her arms wide. "Sadly, that's all I've got. No more insights, no plans to drive the Fangs out. If they're even here. Finn and I didn't come to tell you what to do. This is your land. We respect that. We're here to offer any help you want. We've got more experience with the Fangs and with Wellsprings. What happens next is up to you all. Tell us what to do, and we'll give it our best shot."

That was damned humble, coming from a Dragon. Well, a Dragon's Mate. Rex still found it hard to wrap his head around all of this.

When it was clear that no one meant to take charge, he rose slowly to his feet. "Well, I think the first thing is that we need to figure out if these sippy... uh, zipper..."

"*Sipapus.*"

"...*sipapus* are really magical."

"I can help with that," a Hare replied. "Danielle LaPierre, senior Witch of Sedona. I'll need protection, however."

"Now that's something I *can* do," Donnelly rumbled.

Bree smiled. "Thank you. Mr. Fairburn, could you take us out to some of these sites?"

"Now?" He hesitated, thinking of his kids and a new, untried sitter.

"Yes, if that's possible."

"Sure." This Paige woman seemed fine. In the, er, three minutes he'd talked to her. Damned protective of her boy—which was always a good sign. And his kids were Bear Kin. Tough little buggers. One day with a strange sitter wouldn't kill them.

Hopefully.

Unless she served them eggs over easy....

CHAPTER 5

A shadow crept over Rex as he led the other Shifters out of Cortez.

After the four of them piled into his dusty Jeep, he called home to tell the babysitter he'd be delayed.

No one answered.

Normally, he wouldn't worry. Micah probably conned the poor woman into taking them to Totten. (Because to kids that damned, expensive pool just wasn't as good a leech-filled hole in the ground.) He left a message on the answering machine and headed out for Canyon of the Ancients park.

Yet, a tendril of unease worked its way into his thoughts and nothing he did could banish it. Why hadn't they answered?

Because they're out swimming. Duh.

His Bear growled. He could feel it, shifting from foot to foot, scenting the air. Where were his cubs? Where was his Mate?

Pain shot through him. What the hell was wrong with his damned Bear? Family was the last thing a Bear ought to forget.

My Mate's dead. Remember? Four years ago.

That accusation ought to rouse his Bear's anger—or grief. Instead, it ignored him. Sniffing and sniffing, clawing the ground with agitation. Something was wrong. Something *hunted* his cubs.

Stupidest goddamn idea. Rex gritted his teeth and tightened his grip on the steering wheel.

Bree popped her head between the seats. "Are you okay, Mr. Fairburn?" Her husband, riding in the passenger seat beside him, seemed surprised by that question and peered at him too.

"Fine," he snarled. Damned if he needed some silly Hare fretting over him.

"We can swing by your house if you need to check on something."

"No." His Bear's unrest added a hint of a growl to that word. Donnelly's eyes narrowed.

The Dragon's Mate, however, simply laid a gentle hand on Rex's elbow. That gesture—so kind, so feminine—dumped a bucket of ice water over his anger. "Is your Bear telling you something?"

"Yes, but… well, no. Nothing sensible."

"Stop the car," Donnelly said. Confused, Rex pulled over to the side of the road.

Bree studied him with those strange, witchy eyes of hers. "What's it saying?"

"Stupid things," he stammered. "That something's hunting my kids."

And my 'Mate'—which I don't even have!

Both of the First Flight emissaries stiffened. "That isn't stupid," Donnelly insisted. "We need to find your family, right now."

His Bear roared its agreement, yet Rex hesitated. "Look, guys, I'm not a psychic. I can't know if people are in danger."

"Neither could I," the Dragon replied. "Until, one day, I could. Magic is returning and the world is changing. *We're changing*. Trust your gut. Trust your Bear."

"But they're not answering the phone. I have no idea where they are."

"If you're like me, you don't need to. Your Bear knows. Stop arguing with it and let it go where it wants."

Rex could feel his Bear within him. Pawing the ground, digging sharp tracks with its claws. Anxious to run, to sprint….

…to save.

All right then. Keeping his mind focused so that he didn't truly Shift, he gave his Bear its head.

Show me where they are.

Like a bullet, it shot away. Rex threw the Jeep into gear and tore back onto the road after it. Flying out of Cortez, away from the park entrance. Abandoning the paved roads for a dusty track.

No hesitation, no doubt. His soul was a Bear on a mission.

Both of the Hares hastily buckled their seat belts. Even Donnelly braced himself. "Where are we headed?"

"No idea. Looks like the ass-end of no…."

The word died on his lips as he spotted a car stopped ahead of them. A dozen miles away from anything, a ratty little red Hyundai stood, parked on the side of this cow path.

Why did that scare him? Why did it send his Bear roaring into a frenzy?

Then he saw the birthday balloons in the back seat and knew who owned it.

Paige Hall. His babysitter.

SUN. WATER. STILLNESS, BROKEN ONLY BY SHRIEKS OF JOY.

From her seat in the middle of the picnic blanket, Paige surveyed Sweetwater Hole. When the monsoon season hit, Sweetwater Creek could turn into a frothy, dangerous band of water. Today, under clear skies and a baking sun, it was perfect. A small waterfall had carved a swimming hole and a tiny 'cave', curtained with water. Below that, it slid gently down across algae-covered rocks to another shallow pool.

Micah loved the cave and spent his time diving into the sparkling waters. Meanwhile, the smaller children howled with laughter as they slid to the lower pool, over and over again, like otters.

Little Sam trotted past, tugging at his life vest. Paige caught him as he headed for another slide. "Oops! Let me fix that for you, Sam. It's half fallen off!"

More like 'half pulled-off'. Sam pouted. "Why do I have to wear it? Nobody else does!"

"They're older than you." Carefully, she tightened the straps.

"I'm gonna be five!"

"In six months. So, you're four now."

Sam was not impressed by that logic, and tears welled up in his eyes.

Before he could melt down, she added, "I'll let you swim with me in the big pool in a bit, okay? Once you're a good swimmer, you can take the jacket off."

The promise of a trip to the 'big kids' pool put a smile back on his face. As he darted away, Paige snatched a dangling bit of weed from his bathing suit.

I better run all these suits through the washer before their dad gets back. Sweetwater makes you messy!

But it was fun, such fun. Surrounded by the remains of lunch and cake, Paige leaned back and let the sun's rays caress her face. This was why she'd come here. *This* was where she wanted to raise her son. Leonard and the dangers of Los Angeles seemed to be a world away.

A stealthy movement drew her eye to a pile of rocks across the stream. A coyote stood on it, watching them.

"Oooh, kids, look!" Paige waved them over. "A coyote!"

Jake's eyes grew wide as he hurried over to her side. The other kids didn't much care. Micah ignored the animal completely and even little Nate sniffed, "They're everywhere. We see them in the back yard all the time."

The animal stared at him as he spoke, almost as if it could understand. Then its eyes traveled to Micah and back to her. Something in its stillness, its focus, unsettled her.

"Are coyotes dangerous?" Jake whispered.

"No," Paige assured him. This one seemed freakishly brave, though. As Eden and Nate shrieked their way down the slide once again, it cocked its head and watched them.

Then, slowly and calmly, it strolled down the rocks toward the youngsters.

Paige leaped to her feet. "Eden! Nate! Sam! Over here, now!"

"I thought you said they weren't dangerous!" Jake's eyes went wide with terror.

"They aren't—unless they're sick." No wild animal should be that calm around humans. "Micah! Come here!"

She expected an argument. But when the older boy spotted the coyote and its slow, stealthy approach, he shot through the water and quickly scrambled over to the picnic blanket. So did the little ones. The Fairburn kids had grown up here and knew darn well that no healthy coyote wandered up to people.

A piece of driftwood lay beside the cool waters. Paige snatched it up and retreated back to her cluster of children. "Stay behind me."

The coyote stared at her. Then its tongue lolled out.

Like it was laughing.

"Hey!" Paige screamed at the top of her lungs. "Shoo! Go away!"

It never even flinched. Calmly, it waded into the water.

Micah grabbed a rock and flung it with all his strength. It slammed into the animal's side, staggering it.

The coyote didn't run. It didn't even whimper. With steady, measured steps, it forded the stream.

Rabid. It had to be.

Heart pounding, Paige stepped forward and shielded the children as best she could. Any bite would mean a course of terrible, agonizing shots for its victim. If they fled, the sick creature would run them down long before they reached the car. A sickening thought arose, of the rabid coyote tearing through her tiny charges, snapping and biting.

No. No running. She needed to face it here, to keep it away from the children. If she got bitten… well, she could live with that. But not the little ones. Never them.

Raising her make-shift club, she steeled herself to attack it. To kill something for the first time in her life.

As she did, the coyote's jaw opened.

A thin, reedy voice hissed out of it.

"You are beautiful," the creature whispered. "You feel so much more keenly than these clothes do! I will wear you and we shall feel horrors together."

Shocked, Paige froze. Her mind spun, doubting its own sanity.

Eager now, the coyote trotted forward.

And, as it did, a furious roar shattered the canyon's silence.

A grizzly bear appeared above the falls, barreling forward at a dead run. It launched itself into the air, its speed sending it flying out over the pool.

"Dad!" Micah screamed.

That was when Paige realized that yes, she truly had gone mad.

"Hey!"

His baby-sitter's cry, defiant but tinged with fear, shattered Rex's self-control. It split the air as he jogged… no, sprinted down this path to nowhere.

"Shoo!"

Something threatened her. Something she thought small, a little thing that could be scared off with a few loud words.

His Bear knew better. And it raged.

Fur burst across his body, his teeth grew into fangs. Arms and legs thickened. Without missing a stride he pitched forward, Shifting as he fell. Great clawed paws hit the ground and with a tremendous burst of speed, he raced away from the other Shifters.

Dimly, he heard noises. Paige yelling 'Shoo!' The beat of enormous wings as Donnelly Shifted into his Dragon form behind him.

None of that mattered to Rex, lost in the red fury of Bear mind.

His family was in danger. Nothing was important, nothing existed except that fact.

And the fact that he was going to destroy the threat, whatever it was.

Ahead of him, the creek vanished over a ledge. His sharp ears picked up another faint sound: splashing water not far below.

Good. He flung himself over the edge without pausing. As he plummeted toward the pool, his human half scanned the scene.

His children, clustered together in fear. Paige protecting them, facing down a….

Coyote?

Rex hit the water, sending a wave splashing in all directions. Immediately, his broad paws lashed out and he arrowed through the pool toward her.

A coyote that didn't run was sick. *That* was the danger.

The thing never flinched as he burst out of the pool, water dripping from his thick, brown pelt. Neither did Paige. She stood, frozen, helpless with shock.

Well, she did just get charged by a grizzly. Poor woman probably thinks she's dead.

Except….

She stared, slack-jawed with horror, at the coyote.

Not him.

Who the hell feared a coyote more than a grizzly?

His Bear didn't know and didn't care. One deadly paw lashed out, catching the coyote full on. Its body flipped through the air, spinning, and landed on the other side of the creek with a sickening crunch.

Never whimpering, never crying out.

Rex rose to his hind legs, glowering over at his tiny foe. One leg twitched; the animal still lived. Then a strange black shadow seeped out from under it, spreading like a puddle of oil.

What the hell was that? Rex snuffled, drawing in gulps of air. Bears weren't blind, contrary to folklore, but their sense of smell rivaled a bloodhound's. Even from here, he could pick up the sharp musk of coyote. Mixed with another scent. A dark, rank stench, touched with rot.

Bonk!

Something bounced off his back.

Rex peered around, puzzled.

Paige stood behind him, her face a mask of rage and fear. With a wordless scream of maternal fury, she launched herself at him. Lashing out, time and again, with a thick stick.

Bonk. Bonk. Bonk.

Blows bounced harmlessly off his stomach and chest. Rex had to admire the woman's courage. Here she was, trying to fend off a grizzly bear, with nothing more than a stick.

His Bear, though, was just puzzled.

Why is our Mate attacking us? We saved her.

She's not our 'Mate', he reminded the creature. *And she thinks she just got charged by a grizzly.*

Oh hell, this was a bloody mess. Sure, he was glad he'd put down a rabid coyote, but poor Paige and her kid would be traumatized for life. Rex started to rein his Bear in. Time to shuffle off into the bushes and let his babysitter think she'd driven him off.

Before he could, every child in the gulch stared skyward. Little Jake screamed in panic–and even his own kids shrieked as an enormous white Dragon soared overhead.

Screw Donnelly! What the hell was he thinking? A Bear could be explained, but a Dragon?

And worse was to come. Donnelly banked sharply, sending clouds of dust billowing into the air as his wings beat frantically. Lights burst out around him and he Shifted, dropping to the ground in human form.

"Fairburn! Look out!" he yelled. Pointing *behind* Rex.

At the coyote?

Rex spun, as confused as his Bear.

The coyote lay where he'd thrown it, whimpering. Dying, probably, from a broken back.

But that wasn't what worried Donnelly. The Dragon was pointing at something else. A living shadow that slithered across the desert stones toward him.

The 'oil pool' that spilled out of the dying coyote! It wasn't some liquid or a trick of the light. It was a blob, a foot-long pitch black amoeba scrambling quickly toward him.

"Don't let that thing touch you!" Donnelly bellowed. "They possess people."

For an instant, Rex and his Bear wrestled for control. Subtlety was lost on his Spirit Animal. Was that inkblot a threat? Then it should be destroyed! Chewed, slashed, and raked apart before it could threaten his family! Donnelly's warning meant nothing to it. Don't touch the thing? Ridiculous! How could they kill it without tooth and claw?

Only, Rex remembered magic and it's weird, unpredictable dangers. With an iron will, he forced his Bear back, dragging the raging animal from its 'prey'.

Lights shimmered about him too. Melting down to human form, he spun to face the stunned Paige. "Get the kids out, now!"

He half expected her to faint. Most human minds broke when confronted by a Shift. Mortals panicked, hallucinated, passed out. But his new babysitter possessed an iron spine under her soft, delicate curves. White as a ghost, she staggered to the kids and snatched up little Sam.

His child, not hers. He noted that, warmed that her love protected all children, not just her own.

Time for those thoughts later, not now. "Micah, run!" His oldest dashed away. He and Donnelly snatched up Eden and Jake and charged after him.

Slick and swift as an eel, the darkness chased them. Spilling around boulders, washing across sand. Micah tripped and fell, crying out as he skinned his hands. "Got him!" Rex bellowed. Without breaking stride, he scooped the boy up and tucked him under his arm.

The path back to the Jeep rose sharply out of the gulch. Ahead of him, Paige slipped and nearly fell. Worse, she slowed, forcing Donnelly to pause as well. Rex glanced back, expecting to feel the blob's cold touch on his ankles.

It wasn't even close. It lay at the bottom of the path, as if unwilling to climb any higher. Unmoving, silent. Alien.

The two Hares waited at the top of the falls. Bree immediately echoed Rex's own doubt. "It stopped moving. Why isn't it following?"

In Donnelly's arms, Eden burst into tears. Sam joined her, adding his own thin cry. The Dragon put the girl down gingerly, as if he were afraid she'd break. "It's okay, baby," Rex assured her.

As Hares and Dragon stared down at their strange foe, he and Paige tried to calm the children. Hugs, kisses, and promises that things would be okay took the edge of their hysteria, though they were still petrified.

"What is that thing?" Rex growled.

"I think it's an Adanai," Donnelly said. "A kind of creature from the Other Side. There, they look fae. In this world, they're more like shadows or puddles of ink. And they possess people."

"It said it would wear me," Paige whispered, her face ashen, "and that we would feel horrors together."

The Dragon blinked. "That's messed up. Adanai are assholes… well, some of them. But that's just twisted."

"We have no idea what exists in the spirit world," Bree reminded her husband. "So I wouldn't assume it's an Adanai."

Tremors shook Eden's tiny body. Every inch of his Bear longed to carry her home, someplace she'd be safe. But he couldn't leave a threat like this free in the wilderness where some poor hiker could stumble across it. "Can you watch them a bit longer?" he asked Paige.

Despite all the madness, his babysitter still managed to hold herself together somehow. With a stiff, dazed nod, she pulled his whimpering daughter close. Rex gave the little ones a last round of hugs then slowly, his Bear mourning, he returned to the other Shifters.

Leaving his family in the hands of another.

"So, how do we get rid of this thing?" he demanded. The sooner they dealt with it, the quicker he could go home to his kids.

The Dragon tossed his hands in the air. "No idea."

"I thought you'd fought them before!"

"We did."

"How'd you beat them?"

"The last one avoided me. Took off whenever I showed up."

Something this blob clearly wasn't doing. Though it couldn't climb, it ranged back and forth below them. Its route cut a broad arc across the gully, as if it searched for a path that would lead it to its prey.

Bree glanced back at Paige and lowered her voice. "Your sitter is Kin, right?"

Rex cast a pitying look over his shoulder. "Nope."

Donnelly buried his face in his hands. "Oh, hell. Did I just Shift in front of a mortal again?"

"Yup." Bree shook her head, smiling ruefully. "You have a gift, my love! Look on the bright side, though: at least you didn't stampede this one in front of a car."

"You're never going to let me live that down, are you?" he grumbled.

The four of them watched the creature curl its way across the ravine. "Ideas?" Rex prompted. "Anyone? Danielle?"

"Sorry," the flustered Hare stammered. "I've never seen anything like this."

"How about 'kill it with fire'?" Donnelly suggested. "I always like that one."

"Worth a shot. Just don't start a wildfire. And give me a sec." Rex wandered over to where his sitter and the children waited. "Paige, can you get the kids home? We need to take care of this thing."

"What are you?" she whispered.

Micah answered for him. "Dad's a Bear."

"B-b-but how?"

Rex reached out to give her a reassuring pat–then froze as she flinched. Gently, he took a step back and let his hand drop to his side. "We can talk about this later. I promise, I'll explain. Just protect the kids, okay?"

"All right." Slowly, she herded the children together. Their little cluster straggled down the trail, toward safety. Rex watched until they disappeared over a rise, then returned to the others.

"All clear. Shift away."

Once more, Donnelly transformed into that great white Dragon. He'd seen a few over the years, but the sheer size of the creature, its enormous bulk, took Rex's breath away.

Hope the First Flight's wrong about these Fangs. I'd hate to have to fight a Dragon.

With unexpected grace, Donnelly launched himself into the air. He sailed over the pool, curved back and then, wings beating hard, hovered above the clot of darkness.

It scuttled beneath him. Rex tensed, sure the thing would shock them all and leap to attack. Instead, it remained beneath the Dragon, quivering with excitement.

With a short breath, the Dragon sent a tongue of flame licking across the stones. It washed over the inkblot... to no effect. Their enemy didn't catch fire or even notice as the weeds around it seared to a crisp.

"Damn." Rex sighed as Donnelly flew back and Shifted.

Bree shook her head. "I still don't understand why it won't follow us up here."

Neither did he. And, as he thought about that, Rex noticed another oddity. "Watch the way it travels. It's not moving in a straight line. When it charged me, it came straight on. Now, it keeps curling back and forth."

Like it was trapped inside a glass jar.

Or like a dog running back and forth at the end of a rope...

A rope that was tied to...

"The coyote!" Rex's face lit up. "That thing can't get too far away from it. It's like a dog on a long leash. That's why it's not following us!"

"I think you're right!" Donnelly crowed with delight. Shimmers began to spread across his form. "One fried coyote, coming up."

His wife grabbed him by the elbow before he could Shift. "Wait! Something ties this monster to that coyote. If it's a charm or an amulet, it could give us a clue about who's responsible. And if you destroy it when you burned up that body, we won't know."

That *was* a problem—but Rex had an answer. "I don't think it can jump. Donnelly, why don't you lure it as far away as it can go. I'll come down the other side of the gully."

"And do what? If you pick up some magic amulet it'll be able to follow you."

Rex pulled his phone out of his pocket. "Which is why I'm going to take a picture of it, run, and give you the thumbs up to melt it."

A wide grin split the big Dragon's face. "Sounds like a plan. Anybody with a brain want to lodge a protest? Otherwise, the Bear and I are tag teaming this thing."

"No protest," Bree said with a sigh. "Just be careful."

"Of course. Remember," Rex added, as he jogged off, "for a short distance, Bears can outrun a horse."

The far side of the gully was rougher, lacking the packed trail. He eased himself down as quietly as he could. Climbing back up this would be a bitch, if he had to do it fast. Probably better to just barrel off into the wilderness.

Once more, Donnelly sailed over the ravine. He dipped down, hovering a few feet above the ground. The inkblot scurried beneath him and waited, patient and hungry.

That's my cue.

Quietly, he slipped over to the coyote. To his disappointment, he couldn't see any marks or amulets on the creature's corpse.

No, not 'corpse'. Slowly, almost imperceptibly, the animal's chest rose and fell.

Ah, hell. I didn't quite kill the poor thing.

The kind thing to do was to put it out of its misery. Fortunately, he carried a .357 at all times. (You just never knew when you'd need one. History had taught him trouble didn't always arise in places where it was safe to Shift.) He pulled it out, aimed....

Across the creek, Donnelly snorted loudly. Rex looked up to see the shadow rushing across the water toward him.

With a silent prayer for the coyote, he pulled the trigger. The bullet slammed into the fallen creature.

And, without a sound, the inkblot faded away.

Leaving the Shifters without any clues.

CHAPTER 6

The sun set late this time of year. Yet, worn out by the fear of the attack, the children fell asleep early. Even Jake slumbered, tucked in beside Nate and poor Sam, who refused to be alone in his own bed.

Only Paige remained awake. Pacing. Nervous. Twice, Mr. Fairburn called to warn he was delayed, and to beg her to keep an eye on the kids. She tried to watch tv but ended up staring blindly at the screen, oblivious to the images that flickered across it.

Close to 9:00 pm, lights shined along the driveway and Rex's dusty Jeep rolled up to the house.

Paige turned the tv off and waited.

He entered quietly, taking his shoes off at the door. When he spotted her, he paused, pursing his lips.

"Hi," he mumbled at last.

"Hey."

"Helluva day, right?"

Paige snorted. And suddenly, she was giggling, more from nerves than the joke.

A smile spread across his craggy features, warming the hard lines of his face. "You want a drink?"

"No, thank you." Memories of Leonard were still too fresh, and Paige felt her flash of humor melt away.

Rex didn't notice. He poured himself a double scotch and sat down across from her. "I guess I have a lot to explain."

"You're a Shifter, right? A Bear. Micah told me a lot on the drive back," she admitted.

"I, uh, guess that's good. I've told the kids not to talk about this but, well, I guess today was an exception." He grimaced as the first gulp of scotch burned its way down his throat. Paige found herself growing tense. 'Drinking' meant 'drunk' which meant... very unpleasant things. Leonard had taught her that.

His next taste was smaller, a sip he held and savored. Despite her growing unease, the happiness on his face startled her. Leonard never enjoyed alcohol. The purpose of drinking was to get drunk and once he started, her ex never slowed. He slammed back one drink after another, charging toward a drunken stupor as fast as he could.

As she watched him relish the next mouthful, the knot in her stomach slowly unraveled. Rex wasn't Leonard. With him, maybe there wasn't anything wrong with a drink or two.

Soothed by the scotch's bright touch, the tension drained out of Rex's shoulders. "Micah saved me some work, anyways. Do you have questions?"

"Only one: is he serious? Is the world really full of werewolves and werebears and... and... dragons?"

"Yup. And magic. And witches who turn into Hares."

Crazy... mad... unbelievable... and a hell of a lot better than believing that it was her, not the world, that was insane. Terrifying as it was, she couldn't pretend today hadn't happened. That she hadn't seen strange, impossible, unbelievable things.

Even… beautiful things.

There. Baffling, maddening though it was, she had to admit it was true.

Shifters were beautiful. Terrifying, shocking… and wonderful. Just by their presence, they shredded her dull, mundane world of unpaid bills and soul-less work. Sure, that shadow monster had been a horror. Yet, it had ushered something into her life, something she hadn't felt since she was a little girl.

Mystery. Enchantment.

Magic.

Staring across the coffee table at Rex, she felt a longing stir within her. She wanted to be a part of this craziness. To throw her arms wide and embrace the wildness of it all. Oh, the thought terrified her too. All her life, she'd fled from danger. She'd spent years trying to wrap herself and her son in a cocoon thick enough to keep them safe. Had she been wrong? Had she lost something precious in her fervent fight to avoid risk?

Maybe when you drove risk from your life, all that remained was mush. Life became a safe, boring bowl of oatmeal mush that you had to eat, day after day after day.

Could she push that bowl aside and ask Rex to share his world with her?

Would he want to?

Paige swallowed hard. "I'm sorry I put your children at risk. You must think I'm the world's worst babysitter."

Rex choked on his drink, then booms of laughter burst out of him. "Lady, you attacked a grizzly bear with a stick. You're the best babysitter I've ever had. Well, the ballsiest one, anyway."

The praise brought a flush to her cheeks. "I didn't feel ballsy. I was scared out of my mind."

"As you should have been. Nobody sane stands in front of a pissed-off grizzly and doesn't sweat."

That meant a lot. She found herself smiling, even though he emptied his glass and reached for the bottle again. "What was that thing? Micah didn't know."

"Nobody does. Best guess? Something dark and nasty from the Other Side."

"What's that?"

"Some people call it the Spirit World. Supposed to be another universe parallel to ours. They say that Shifters' animal souls came from there, once upon a time." Rex shrugged and toasted her with his new glass. "Don't know if any of that is true. Honestly, I didn't believe in the Other Side before today. But that blob made a convert out of me."

"Is it dead?"

"It's gone. It needed a host and when we killed that coyote it lost its grip on this world."

That would be a relief… except for the obvious questions. "How did it get here? Is it coming back?"

"No idea," he admitted. "We searched the ravine and couldn't find anything out of the ordinary."

"Not even at the ruins?"

His head snapped up and he stared at her with his intense brown eyes. "What ruins?"

"They don't have a name and they're not on any map. Jake and I found them on our last trip to Sweetwater. Up over a rise, maybe a quarter mile from the swimming hole."

Rex bounded to his feet, drink forgotten. "That's it! It's got to be! Somebody–we don't know who–has been screwing around at ruins in this area. Looks like they're trying to do some kind of magic ritual. I bet they succeeded at Sweetwater."

"Tomorrow," he added, "can you show us where those ruins are?"

And there it was: her invitation to this new world. Cheeks flushed, Paige nodded. "Of course! I'd be happy to!"

Until, suddenly, the old world struck back. "Oh crap. I can't. I have to work."

He laughed, throwing his arms wide. "I'm your boss. I give you the day off."

A kind offer, but she winced. "I can't. I really need the money. Things are... not good for Jake and me right now."

"What's wrong?" He sat down on the couch next to her. Heat radiated off him, a strong, masculine warmth that sent a shiver of pleasure through her.

"A few months ago, we had to leave Los Angeles quickly. I had enough cash to rent a small place, but we left most of our stuff behind. Been hard to replace things."

"Why the rush?" The brush of his hand against her thigh sent her thoughts scattered like startled doves.

"It... it was complicated."

He caught her chin in his firm grasp and tilted it up, breaking her free of that welling shame. Intent, patient, he studied her with concern. She found herself staring back, caught by details. The flecks of gold that brightened his brown eyes. The faint shadow of a beard darkening his square jaw and broad, handsome cheeks. Nothing was small or delicate about him. From the bulge of his muscled arms to the wide planes of his face and the hard, Roman line of his nose, he was a big, *big* man.

Paige found herself wondering if other parts of him were as generously endowed. A thought that set her cheeks alight with desire.

"Tell me," he urged, mistaking her blush for something more innocent.

"It's a long, ugly story," she stammered. "The short version is, I have lousy taste in men."

"Did he hurt you?"

She could hear it then. The Bear that lurked inside of him. A hint of its growl echoed behind those words.

Any sane woman would be terrified to know that the man sitting beside her, touching her, wasn't fully human. An animal, a predator, lived inside him. Something wild and dangerous.

Yet, the emotion that set her heart racing wasn't fear.

How could that be? All her life, she'd been afraid. Of her strict, domineering father. Of Leonard. Of muggers and strange noises and sudden laughter on the streets at night. Now, when she sat inches away from the first truly dangerous thing in her short life, she was free from fear's weakening touch.

Why?

A memory rose. Rex, rearing up between her and the shadow monster. A shaggy mountain of protective rage, shielding her and the children. Willing to lay down his life to save the innocent.

How could she fear a love like that? The form it took—Bear or human–meant nothing. Love was beautiful, no matter what it looked like.

He leaned even closer and her lips parted as he hesitated, inches away from them. "You can tell me."

Tell him what? Oh! Lost in admiration of his powerful, magnificent body, she'd completely forgotten his question!

"Um, yes," she stammered. "He did hurt me. Though only toward the end."

A thumb, rough from hard work, caressed her cheek. "How could anyone do that to someone so beautiful?"

His kindness… the gentle shock of his words… the desire she saw burning in his face… they merged, creating a heady, sweet brew. Intoxicated by it, she leaned forward and kissed him.

Lips, warm and welcoming, met hers, sending a shock of electric pleasure coursing through her body. And he returned her kiss with a hunger of his own. A hand caught her, pulled her close, and she felt strong fingers wind through her short curls.

But even as her body yielded to his urgent, demanding touch, her mind rebelled.

Rex is my boss. I'm kissing my boss.

"I'm sorry." She broke away from the pleasure of his touch, trembling with the force of her need. "I shouldn't have done that. I...."

He kissed her again, silencing her protest with proof of his desire. She had awakened the Bear and it was too late to turn back.

Not that she truly wanted to. Behind her feeble words, her body urged him on. Her mouth, welcoming, eager. Her arms wound about his muscular shoulders. Her breasts, nipples stiffening as she pressed against his chest.

I should say something... I should stop him... this won't end well....

No. She swept those mewling doubts aside. No mixed messages. She wanted him and she wouldn't pretend she didn't. She didn't care what anyone said. Not her parents, not Leonard, not the rest of the housecleaning staff at Ancient Ways. She wanted Rex Fairburn–and he wanted her too.

Nothing else mattered.

Arms like steel beams lowered her to the couch. Their lips, still locked in passion, never stopped exploring each other. He bent down, shifting closer. The hint of his weight pressed against her, a delicious prison from which she never wanted to escape. One leg slipped between hers, the rough cloth of his jeans rubbing against the crotch of her pants. She wrapped her legs around it, pulling it close. Letting its strength, its heat, tease her womanhood.

His hand slipped under her shirt, skimming lightly across the soft skin of her belly. It rose, seeking her breasts. The lacy cloth of her bra taunted him, denying him the secrets he lusted after. Her nipples came alive as those fingers sought them, stroking, squeezing. Then he caught the band of the bra and pushed it upward, freeing the pert globes of her breasts.

Paige moaned at their freedom and arched her back, surrendering herself to him. Having won its first 'battle', that roguish hand caught her shirt and pushed it up too. Soft cotton whispered across her bare breasts, their touch breathing on the flames of her passion, fanning them into a hotter blaze.

And then, he broke away from her, leaving her aching, yearning for the return of the sweet taste of his mouth. That pain lasted only for a second, though. Then those lips touched her belly in a hungry, reverent kiss. She moaned as his mouth rose, seeking the curves of her breasts. Teasing lips sucked eagerly, a sly tongue lashed her nipples, sending a wave of pure ecstasy sweeping through her. Her body burned, possessed by some primal, animal nature. Helpless beneath him, she writhed, thrusting her breasts against his face, rubbing herself against the hard, unyielding strength of his leg.

As her passion flared higher, a sound broke through it.

A door clicking open.

The pad of small feet.

Like a pair of scalded cats, she and Rex scrambled apart. As Paige yanked her shirt down, little Eden appeared in the hallway.

"Uh, hem," Rex coughed. "Hi, sweetie. Trouble sleeping?"

"Mmm." The child stomped into the bathroom and closed the door.

Stiff and silent, the pair of them sat a foot apart, waiting for the sound of a flush. Eden reappeared, tottering back toward her room with the focus of a tiny zombie.

"Night, baby!" her father called. The girl didn't answer.

A second click told them when they were alone again. But though her body burned with unfulfilled need, the interruption had shredded the mood.

Worse, it had given her time to think, and regret.

"I'm sorry. I shouldn't have started this."

Eyes twinkling, Rex rose to his feet and offered her a hand up. Paige took it, heart sinking. Knowing that it was time for her to collect her son, trudge home… and spend the night burning with unmet needs.

Her boss had other ideas, however. When she stood, he didn't release her hand. Instead, he pulled her toward the sliding glass doors that opened onto the backyard. "Hang on. I want to show you something."

Meekly, she followed him outside and around to the pool. Submerged lights filled its depths with a sapphire glow.

"Do you know what this is?" he asked her.

"Um, a pool?"

"No." He waved his arms wide, taking in the pool, the sauna, the slide and lounge chairs. "This is a child-free zone."

She could see where *this* was leading, and she giggled. "Your pool is a child-free zone?"

"Yes. Even if one of my kids wakes up in the middle of the night with a desperate need to go swimming, they will not come here. They will go to my bedroom and start whining that I need to take them to Totten Reservoir."

"Why? What's wrong with the pool?"

"I have *no* idea," he grumbled, as he turned to her with a

mischievous grin of his own. "Want to go for a swim with me and try to solve that mystery?"

Why yes, yes, she did! It would beat the hell out of going home frustrated. But... "I didn't bring a bathing suit."

"Good."

Without a word more, he shucked off his clothes and tossed them aside.

And just like that, her hunger came roaring back as she gazed at his naked body in all of its splendor.

Rex Fairburn was a big man. Stripped of his clothes, it became clear that not one ounce of that was flab. Broad shoulders, long legs circled by bands of muscle. A barrel chest covered with soft brown hair. And his manhood... Roused, it swelled from between his legs. Inviting her to finish awakening it.

He was a giant of a man. Nature hadn't shorted him in *any* part. Her breath fluttered at the thought that this man, this mountain, would be hers.

Stairs descended into the shallow end of the pool. Rex waded down until the glittering waters hid his manhood from her. "Coming?"

Oh, she wanted to. She did. Yet, she hesitated. No fence shielded the pool from prying eyes. The desert surrounded them, sweeping away in all directions.

The kids... the neighbors will see...

What neighbors? Moonlight softened the harsh badlands into a silvery wilderness–one where not a single light broke through the darkness. Rex owned all the land around them. And the kids? All of the bedrooms faced the open desert. *Not* the pool.

No one could see. No one would be shocked.

She could do what she wanted.

And what she wanted was to join him.

Logic assured that her modesty was safe. Yet, an irrational

feeling lingered as she stripped. A titillating, mischievous notion that she was doing something shocking. Something delightfully scandalous.

Cool night air surrounded her as she shed her shirt and jeans. Bra and underwear joined them, and then she stood, free in the moonlight. Unhindered by clothes. For all of her life, nakedness had shamed her. It was something to be hidden in bathrooms and behind locked doors. Now, she stood feeling like a goddess as she surveyed the land around them.

And Rex watched her in delight and wonder, offering her the adoration that a goddess deserved. His eyes traveled the curves of her body, pausing on her breasts and the short fuzz between her legs. When they rose, at last, to meet her gaze, they were filled with marvel and a desire, a lust, that took her breath away.

No man had ever looked at her with such naked hunger, such a powerful need.

A need as strong as her own. One she could no longer deny.

Pale under the moon's silvery rays, she strode to the steps. Letting him enjoy the sway of her hips, the bob of her breasts. As she took the first step, water closed over her ankles, still holding echoes of the day's relentless heat. Deeper she waded, until she stood by Rex's side.

"Damn, you are gorgeous," he whispered.

With a beckoning smile, she strode past. "Shall we find out what's 'wrong' with this pool?"

Water enfolded her, buoying her and swallowing her. Under its touch, her breasts rose. Paige flipped onto her back and began to slowly swim. She loved the view of Rex and the feel of the water swirling across her bare skin. How different it felt to glide through a pool naked, free from the damp, clinging cloth of a bathing suit.

In her wake, Rex followed with strong, sure strokes. On each, his arm broke the surface, water coursing along the bands of its muscles. He shot forward, catching her, passing her. When she reached the end of the pool, he waited.

This time when he pulled her close, no foolish cloth kept their bodies apart. Once more, their mouths joined, lips and tongues woven close in exploration. Every inch of her body sang with joy. Slick with water, her arms slid across his muscles as she hugged him. Her breasts pressed against the damp hair of his chest. Only their legs stayed apart, tasked with the chore of keeping them afloat.

That distance chafed her, teased her. Time and again, she felt the brush of his naked manhood across her skin. Slipping across her thighs, the peach fuzz between her legs. At each touch, her breath caught in her throat. It tantalized her, drove her mad with need.

And yet, swimming, that need remained unfulfilled.

With a groan, Rex broke away and headed toward shallower water. Before, the pace had been leisurely, the swim a chance to admire the other's body. Now, both of them drove hard, urged on by hunger and an inescapable need.

He reached shallower water first. As his feet found the ground, he turned, holding a hand out to her. Paige caught it and he pulled her toward him. She was flying, sailing through the water, to be caught up in his arms.

Brawny arms closed around her, folding her into his passionate, unbreakable grip. Once more, she twined her arms around his neck and kissed him, her breasts pressed close to the wet curls of his chest. Beneath the water, she felt his manhood. Eager, aroused, nuzzling against her most private parts. Fire blazed through her at its insistent touch. A hunger, a yearning, like nothing she had ever felt.

One hand slid down the soft, wet skin of her back. Caught in his arms, she felt a hand explore her body. The round curves of her buttocks. The flat lines of her thighs. Inquisitive fingers traced a path across them, kneading, massaging.

His other hand joined the exploration. They paused, cupping the globes of her buttocks. Then, with a swift, fluid motion, he lifted her from her feet.

Held, she floated. Free, yet somehow helpless, a delicious, intoxicating set of opposites. Paige surrendered herself to it. To his strength and power. To trust. As he pulled her near, she wrapped her long legs around his hips.

Deep, shuddering breaths shook his broad chest as he fought to rein his passion in. The rock-like shaft of his manhood pressed between her legs, eager, no longer willing to be denied. Rex lifted her, staring up with adoration. Then slowly, gently, he lowered her onto himself.

She felt him slide inside her. Filling her, taking her. More and more until she took the full length of his enormous cock.

A moan escaped her, a primal sound of animal need and her legs tightened, pulling him deeper into her secrets.

That cry unleashed his Bear.

With a roar of delight, he threw control to the wind and surrendered to his passion.

Hard, sure thrusts sent his cock gliding through her willing body. Each one stoked the fire blazing within her. Paige moaned, urging him on with her wordless, aching need. Blind with hunger, she clawed at his shoulders, his short hair. With each stroke, her legs squeezed tight, joining him in his fierce hunger.

Tremors rippled through his muscled body as he fought to hold himself back from the edge, unwilling to surrender completely until he was sure that she had reached the pinnacle.

When she did, she threw her head back and wailed, a cry of pure pleasure offered to the moon above. Hearing her, the last of his restraint shattered. Faster, harder, the thrusts came. Each lash drove her ecstasy higher, held it for yet one more second. She found herself floating in his arms, filled with him, feeling that moment of wordless delight linger on and on.

With a rush, he came, filling her with his seed. A groan of fulfillment slipped from his lips. One moment longer, he held her. Sated at long last. Feeling beautiful, loved, fulfilled in a way that no lover had ever offered. Reveling in the fading touch of that ecstasy.

Gently he pulled himself free. Paige found her footing again and glanced up at him, proud and dazed.

Above them the moon gazed down, beaming its approval.

CHAPTER 7

When Paige awoke the next morning, the bed was empty. Warmth lingered on the sheets where Rex had slept; he hadn't been gone long. It was early. She stretched her hand out, fingers spread, enjoying the fading trace of his presence.

How long had it been since she made love? Sure, she'd had sex with Leonard. But that wasn't the same thing at all. 'Love' with Leonard meant waiting long hours, alone, unsure if he'd be able to make love when he got back from the bar… or if he'd be so drunk that he'd stagger to bed and pass out, face down in the pillows. If he did manage to stay awake, sex was quick and fumbling. A clumsy joining that satisfied his needs, yet left her aching and hungry.

Last night, finally, that hunger was sated. *That* deserved the phrase 'making love'. Passion, longing, desire. Raised to a fever pitch she'd never felt. Every promise fulfilled, utterly and completely. A lover who made her feel like a woman, a creature of beauty and mystery. Rex had adored her, devoured her with a hunger that matched her aching needs.

Yet, as she reluctantly slipped out of bed and found yesterday's clothes, doubts remained. Rex was her *boss*. That was kind of creepy. Paige wasn't even sure she wanted to be in a relationship now, so soon after fleeing Leonard. And there were red flags too. The way Rex tossed back so much scotch without flinching. The realization that she was just a babysitter, not the type of woman that a millionaire developer fell for. The fact that Bears weren't safe–as yesterday proved. Did she really want to expose her son to things like that blob?

Only one thing was clear to her.

I can't laugh at Judy for running off to Denver with some guy from a party! I'm as hopeless as she is.

Time to stop over-thinking this. Paige stepped out of the bedroom to see what the day would bring.

REX LOUNGED IN HIS STUDY SCANNING EMAIL, A STEAMING mug of coffee beside him. Morning sunlight cast a golden glow across his brown hair, raising an echo of last night's desire. But as he glanced up at her, the coolness in his face chilled her.

"Good morning Miss Hall."

So that was how it was. "Good morning Mr. Fairburn."

Immediately, he shook his head. "Paige. Sorry, we're a bit beyond titles now."

"We are." She smiled softly, hoping that she would break the sheen of frost that cooled the room.

Rex only grew more distant. "Look, I'm sorry about last night. I took advantage of you and I shouldn't have done that."

"No, you didn't." A dull grief settled over her as she felt the night's silly dream die. "I wanted it too."

"You need to know that I'm not looking for a relationship."

"Neither am I," she assured him. She wasn't sure that that was true, but saying it made it feel right.

The chill in the room faded as he sighed with relief. "Good. I'm relieved that we're on the same page. I just didn't want any misunderstandings."

"Last night was fun." What a shallow, trivial way to describe the most ecstatic night of her life! Yet Paige forced the words out. "I know it's not going to happen again, though."

Rex nodded. For one moment, they stood, wrapped in an awkward silence. Finally, he cleared his throat and asked, "Would you like some coffee?"

"Yes, please."

And with that dull, boring question, life fell back into its depressing rut. Time to face facts. No millionaire lover would sweep her off her feet. She was a house cleaner and a babysitter. No more Shifters and magic for her.

And no more danger. Remember that. You have to think of Jake.

Caffeine helped her mind throw off the last mists of sleep and ridiculous dreams. As she sipped, Rex explained the day's plan. They'd meet Danielle and the Donnellys out by Sweetwater and head to the ruins. At the first sign of danger, the Dragon would get her out to safety.

"That's fine." Danger wasn't as scary when it was aimed at her, rather than her son.

The kids would stay here, under the care of Mrs. Gordon.

Her supervisor? *That* felt like biting tin foil.

When she winced, Rex shrugged. "Sorry. I really *am* hard up for decent sitters. She's the only person I could get on short notice."

Great. Now everyone at Ancient Ways would know she'd slept with the boss. Sadly, she didn't have any other suggestions. Judy was still in Denver and she didn't know many people here.

"There's one other thing." Rex pulled a thick envelop out of his desk and handed it to her.

Inside were hundred dollar bills. Twenty or thirty of them.

Nausea twisted Paige's guts. She flung the envelope back onto his desk, cheeks blazing. "I don't want your money."

"Don't be silly," the Bear growled. He retrieved the envelope and held it out once more. "You need this."

Paige back away. "I *told* you that I wanted last night too. You don't need to pay me."

His eyes widened in horror, a look of shock so profound that it dulled the sharp edge of her outrage. "No! That's not what this is! I didn't mean... I'm not trying to pay you for... for anything. But you mentioned that you were having money troubles and I want to help."

She folded her arms across her chest. "I prefer to earn my money."

And still he stood there, waving that wad of cash at her. "Dammit, woman, don't be so proud."

All that did was make her chin rise. "When you're poor, pride and honor are all you've got. I'm not giving them up."

"I know. I wasn't born rich." His arm fell to his side, but he didn't let go of the envelope. "I started out working at a food cart when I was a teen. Saved up enough to buy my own cart... then a restaurant... then a rental property. And, well, it went from there." Calm and level, he met her gaze. "But I'm no stranger to hard work and the strength it takes to pull yourself up by your bootstraps."

"Then you know why I can't accept that."

"I won't try to force you to take it," he said. Ignoring the fact that that was exactly what he was doing! "But look at this from my point of view. I know you're struggling. I know I can help you without any effort—this money doesn't mean anything to me. Yet you won't let me help."

"Do you hand out thousands of dollars to every poor stranger you meet?"

"You're not a stranger." A heat entered his words, a distant echo of last night's passion. "I admit I don't want a girlfriend. I don't even know you well. But I do care for you."

One word, one tiny confession of feelings, and her traitorous heart melted.

"What I saw yesterday told me everything I need to know about you. You're brave and smart. You're a fantastic mother, a woman who would die to save innocent children. You have the soul of a mother Bear, even if you aren't a Shifter. I admire you, and I would consider it an honor if you would let me help you."

Kind words didn't change anything; charity was still a hand-out. Yet looking at him, seeing the kindness and affection in his eyes, Paige felt her resistance crumble. "Well it… it would help, I admit. Moving was expensive. And we had to leave without most of our things, so…"

Rex held the envelope out again. This time she took it. "Someday I'm going to ask you what happened. Why you had to flee your last home. But," he sighed, "we've got enough on our plate today. Let's take care of them first, shall we?"

WHEN MRS. GORDON ARRIVED TO WATCH THE KIDS, HER supervisor was every bit as shocked and titillated as she'd feared. To add to her anguish, Jake hated to be left with strangers and promptly melted down. His teary eyes followed her as they drove away, filling Paige with guilt.

If there was *any* chance of meeting another blob, though, she was keeping her son far away.

The Donnellys waited at the Sweetwater trailhead,

sipping coffee and munching on donuts. With everyone here, the group headed out across the desert. The trail ended at the little swimming hole. Sometime during the night, raccoons had discovered the remains of their picnic lunch. Plastic plates and bits of birthday cake lay scattered about.

Paige's nose wrinkled. Good thing she hadn't wanted any leftovers! Yesterday's 'monster attack' might have erased the memory of Jake's terrible 'party'… but it certainly didn't improve the day!

As Finn collected the basket and blanket, Paige surveyed the countryside to get her bearings. "Ridge with a funny rock… gully to the left… okay, this way guys!"

With that, she headed out into the trackless wilderness.

The look of shock on Rex's face almost made her laugh. "Uh, where's the trail?"

"There isn't one."

"Then how do you know where to go?"

"Jake and I visited it a couple times."

Bree and Finn seemed as puzzled as the Bear. "How could you even know it's out here?" the Hare asked.

"That's what our family does for fun: we look for old ruins."

"You wander around the desert. With your son." Rex clearly doubted her sanity.

"With my son. And topo maps, GPS, a compass, and *tons* of water. Mostly, we follow gullies like this one. They're signs that there used to be water here. And where there's water, there's life. All Ancestral Puebloan sites were near water."

"So, you're an archeologist?" Bree asked.

"Not a real one, no. I never went to college. But I've always adored Puebloan ruins. That's why Jake and I moved out here. My parents took me to Mesa Verde when I was a kid and I've loved them ever since."

The route up the gully was filled with rocks and gravel, making the footing treacherous. Silence fell as people minded their feet. A few minutes later, Paige pointed at a small landslide marked with footprints. "That's how we get up."

A quick scramble brought them to a small plateau. Low stone walls, the remains of a little village, lay scattered about. "Not very impressive, but this is it."

Bree glanced about. "Is there a kiva here?"

"Yup." Once more, Rex seemed surprised by her knowledge. As if she wouldn't know what an Ancestral Puebloan holy site looked like! "Over here."

When the Hare spotted the circular walls, her eyes lit up. "Ahah! This is an old one!"

Paige started to step carefully over the walls when Rex caught her arm. "Keep back. If that thing came from here, it could be dangerous."

Oh, right. Reality came crashing back. They weren't out on a weekend stroll. They were hunting monsters. And Bree and Danielle immediately confirmed Rex's worries. "Magic," both Hares blurted out, in unison. "Strong."

Mouth dry, Paige retreated to a rock and sat down.

The four Shifters went to work. The Hares inched closer, staring and sniffing before each step. Dragon and Bear hovered a short distance behind, alert for any danger. A half hour passed before they crossed twenty feet, and the sun grew hot overhead.

Finally, Bree gave the okay sign. "All clear. I don't think it's dangerous."

Curious, Paige drifted closer. The others clustered around something. Probably the *sipapu*, if she remembered the ruin right.

"So, ladies, what are we looking at?" Finn glanced at the two Hares.

"A gate," Danielle replied. "A door to the Other Side."

Rex whistled. "So, *sipapus are* Wellsprings!" Paige wasn't sure what that meant, but this didn't seem like the time to ask.

Bree shook her head. "Not exactly. Wellsprings allow magic to flow through. This thing doesn't. In fact, there's a faint flow *into* it."

"And those markings?" The Bear pointed down.

The Hares traded glances then shrugged. "I don't know," Bree confessed. "I'm going to take some pictures and ask a friend who specializes in the archeology of magic. She may be able to decipher them."

As she did that, Rex waved Paige over. "Were these things here the last time you visited?"

Stepping to his side, she glanced down at the *sipapu*, the ritual pit found in most kivas. Her stomach flopped when she said that no, it had been vandalized. Someone had scratched a rectangle on its bottom. Runes ringed it, and the sides of the box were slashed with dozens of short, straight lines.

Worst of all was the color. "Is that blood?" she whispered.

"I think so."

"No, none of this was here. This was just a hole two weeks ago."

"So, let me get this straight," Rex said, his face grim. "Some time in the last two weeks, someone hiked out to an unknown Puebloan ruin. They carved this crap on it, reddened it with blood, and… what? Summoned a demon?"

"A spirit," Danielle corrected him. "Something from the Other Side."

The five of them stared at the defiled kiva until Finn cleared his throat. "Are there a lot of these ruins in the Four Corners region?"

"Hundreds," Rex said. "Maybe thousands."

The Dragon grimaced. "Most of them are known, though, right?"

Paige shook her head sadly. "Nope. Very few, actually. The majority are just out there, somewhere."

"Ah hell," Finn groaned. "This is going to be a crap-ton of work."

CHAPTER 8

*R*ex and the Shifters might have a ton of work before them–but so did Paige. And it was crappy, soul-killing work.

Despite the unnerving events of the weekend, Monday morning began like every other workday. Get up early and make breakfast for herself and a subdued, quiet Jake. Drop her son off with Judy (who gulped coffee at a tremendous rate and babbled endlessly about Denver). Then coax her battered Hyundai back onto the road, praying it wouldn't be the car's last trip.

She parked in the back lot at Ancient Ways, in a distant corner where no wealthy patron would be affronted by the sight of her derelict car. Slipped in the rear door and checked in with housekeeping.

As she'd feared, Mrs. Gordon waited for her. Lips pinched. Disapproval radiating from every line of her wrinkled face. "Miss Hall. You're on time. How surprising. I feared your 'big weekend' might wear you out."

"No ma'am." The insult stung, but Paige didn't rise to the

bait. Meek and quiet, she took her room assignments and headed out, pushing her cleaning cart before her.

The morning passed slowly as she worked her way through an endless string of dirty rooms. Beds to make. Toilets to clean. Rugs to vacuum. Again and again, each room exactly like the other. Except for the handful that weren't, where some guest had made a truly disgusting mess. Which *she* had to clean up.

Room 415 was one of *those* rooms. The earthy scent of pot hit Paige as soon as she opened the door–onto a scene of devastation. Bottles lay scattered everywhere. Several had tipped over on the bureau, dribbling beer and whiskey down its side. Garbage and the remains of room service lay scattered about. Worst of all, a glance at the bathroom revealed that at least one person had missed the toilet entirely.

Welcome to my life.

Opening a window, Paige gritted her teeth and got to work. 415 was a horror and would throw her schedule completely off. But standing here gagging didn't help.

Start with the worst, right? Gloves on, mop and clean the bathroom. After that, the rest of the work would all be downhill. That was the theory anyway. But when she turned to the 'easy' chore (making the beds) she found that life had left her a little surprise. One of 415's guests had vomited on a pillow then kicked it away.

Paige stared at the soiled pillow and at the smear staining the wall, and then she counted to ten.

I need this job... I need this job... I need this job...

When the urge to quit faded away, she stripped the bed and fetched a spare pillow from the closet.

Each room at Ancient Ways came with a good-sized closet. 415's was full to the brim. A large object filled it, high as her chest and covered by a sheet.

Weird. And none of her business, but....

Paige popped her head into the hall. Seeing no one, she returned to the closet and peeked under the cover.

The mysterious object wasn't one big thing. It was a huge stack of plastic totes. Half were empty, half filled with packing peanuts. One, on the top, was only partially full. Curious, she popped the lid and glanced inside.

A dozen tiny animal carvings lay on top of the peanuts, each in its own plastic bag. Next to them, the edge of a pot stuck out of the packing. Black spirals and lines swirled across its pale grey surface.

Zuni fetishes and Puebloan pots! Paige's eyes widened in shock. *This is a fortune in antiquities!*

But where was the documentation? The papers that described where the item had been found? Any legitimate collector demanded that.

Only thieves didn't care. Her heart skipped a beat as she pawed through the tote. No papers, no tags to identify the individual objects. Just valuable 'stuff' tossed in boxes.

'Stuff' taken from sites like the Sweetwater ruins.

This couldn't be a coincidence! Shivering, she covered the boxes and backed out. Rex needed to know. Maybe these were the people who summoned that demonic thing that attacked them. She needed to call him....

But for that, she needed his phone number. Why hadn't she asked for it?

Because that seemed wrong after...well, what happened. If he wanted to talk to me again, he would have offered it.

Not a problem. Paige knew someone who *could* call the Bear.

"MRS. GORDON!"

Her supervisor frowned at Paige over the day's paper-work. "Miss Hall. Surely, you're not done already?"

"No, but there's a problem with 415."

"And I expect *you* to clean that problem up!" the woman hissed. "Yes, yes, I know they're messy. Candy and Sara both whined about them last week. But *they* did their jobs. Something I expect from you, too, no matter who you think you are."

Once more, Paige clenched her teeth and ignored the jibe. "You don't understand. They're stealing Indian artifacts. Their closet is full of them!"

Mrs. Gordon's eyes lit with outrage. Aimed, unfortunately, at the wrong target. "What were you doing rifling through guests' belongings? Why, I should call the police on you!"

"I had to get a pillow and I...I saw them."

"How do you know they're not legal?" her boss sniffed.

"They don't have proper papers."

"Oh really? And you just saw that? Without digging through a guest's belongings?"

Okay, that was a problem. But so what? If she'd uncovered the people behind that blob, Rex wouldn't care about little details like that.

"You need to call Mr. Fairburn and tell him."

"Do I?" A faint smirk curled the corners of the woman's lips. "Why? Didn't he give you his number? How strange."

Each insult felt like a slap in the face. "Listen, we went hiking yesterday, and Rex... Mr. Fairburn was very worried about people stealing pots from Indian ruins. You need to let him know."

Mrs. Gordon folded her arms and scowled. "Call the police if you think they're stolen. Just don't expect me to vouch that you're not a thief."

"*LISTEN TO ME!*" Paige screamed.

Both of them fell silent, shocked by her outburst. An urge to run, to flee this embarrassment, welled up within her, but

Paige refused to back down. "You're going to call Mr. Fairburn, right now, and tell him about this. If you don't, I will stop by his house and tell him myself. And I will also tell him that it was *you* who withheld this information from him!"

Eyes narrowed, fuming, Mrs. Gordon glared at her. Paige began to fear that the woman would call her bluff. That she'd have to walk out of her job–the job she desperately needed. In the end, though, her supervisor rose stiffly to her feet. "As you will, *Miss* Hall."

She retreated to her office, slamming the door behind her. A minute later, Paige heard the buzz of her voice, too low to understand. Hard as it was, she forced herself to wait.

When her boss stepped out, the disdain on her face sent Paige's heart plummeting. "Mr. Fairburn says not to worry about 415. He knows the guests and is aware of their collection. Their *legitimate* collection."

That couldn't be! Even an amateur like her knew you didn't just rip pots out of the ground and toss them in boxes.

"But...."

"No 'buts'," Mrs. Gordon yelled, her thin voice rising to a screech. "Now get back to work. Or quit. Personally, I don't care which you do."

Dazed, Paige trudged back to the fourth floor. This couldn't be right. Rex wouldn't support this kind of thievery, would he?

Though....

How well did she really know him? Being a good... no, a fantastic lover didn't make a man trustworthy.

No, she couldn't believe that. The pride in his voice when he praised her 'bravery'... the outrage in his face when he saw the defiled *sipapu*. That couldn't be fake.

Maybe he just didn't understand. Maybe Mrs. Gordon made it sound like 415 had taken a couple of pot shards rather than a hundred priceless artifacts. With pictures she could go over tonight....

...and see him again....

That thought, unbidden, brought a flush of warmth to her face. A heat very different from the burning shame that Mrs. Gordon summoned.

Well, yes, she'd see him again. Briefly. And she could show him that this was serious.

She had to clean 415 anyway. That, or lose her job.

The whole, huge, steaming mess waited for her as she re-entered the room. At least fresh air had taken the edge off the stench of pot and pee. Paige closed the door. It seemed a reasonable precaution, even if the cleaning staff wasn't supposed to do it. Then she opened the closet, took the lid off the top tote, and dug her phone out of her pocket.

"What the hell are you doing?" growled a low, menacing male voice.

Right behind her.

Paige shrieked and the phone tumbled to the floor.

One of the 415 guests had returned—and he *wasn't* happy to see her pawing through his stuff. At first glance, he didn't look threatening. Neat blue polo shirt, white cotton pants, a nice pair of leather shoes. Nothing to set him apart from the other guests of Ancient Ways. Sure, the arms revealed by that shirt boasted ripped, wiry muscles. Still, he could have been any of the New Age tourists that flooded the resort's halls.

Until you looked into his eyes. Rage filled them. Violence and a boundless fury that twisted his lips into a feral snarl.

Under that stare, Paige froze like a deer in headlights. All of her plans and her carefully plotted lies scattered like dandelion seeds in the wind. "C-c-cleaning?" she gulped.

"Bullshit." And suddenly, there was a gun in his hand, summoned from some hidden holster. Paige's knees grew weak as he raised it and pointed it at her face. "Who sent you?"

"No one! I mean, housekeeping! I'm the cleaning lady!"

"Then why are you taking pictures of my stuff?"

"Because they're, uh, pretty?"

415 didn't believe that for a second. "Last chance. Start telling the truth or they're going to find your body on the side of the highway."

Terror flooded through her, threatening to wash away all rational thought and send her screaming for the door. In its wake, though, came a bitter, twisted thought. One that almost made her laugh.

And I came here because it was 'safer' than LA.

"What's so funny?"

Lord, she was a terrible actor! Desperate, she seized the only 'weapon' she had. "You. If you knew what was good for you, you'd be running right now."

Her vague threat only amused him. "Uh huh. Why?"

He *had* to be tangled up in all of this mess, and if he was, he *had* to be a Shifter. So….

Summoning her few rags of courage, Paige straightened and glared back at him. "Before I came up here, I called Rex Fairburn. He's on his way now. And when he gets here, Rex will tear you apart."

" 'Rex.'" Her captor's sneer deepened. "You're on a first name basis with your boss, huh?"

"I am."

"Girlfriend? Nah, he wouldn't make a woman he cared for clean rooms. Mistress?" Paige blushed at the contempt in that word. "Gotcha. Mistress."

"When he shows up–"

"Shut up, woman. You didn't call him."

"That's not true!"

"If you had, you wouldn't be here." Patience dripped from

his words, but that gun never wavered. "Mr. Fairburn would have told you to mind your own business. He's our partner."

That was almost what Mrs. Gordon had said! Paige felt the world tilt beneath her feet. Was Rex truly a villain? He'd seemed so shocked by the vandalism they saw. That couldn't be an act... could it?

Her heart said no.

Then again, she was a lousy judge of men. Why should Rex be any better than Leonard?

415 grinned at the shock in her face. "That's what I thought. You stepped in this shit all on your own. Probably trying to impress Fairburn or something stupid like that. Okay, so listen. If you do exactly what I tell you, you'll get out of this alive. I would prefer not to shoot Fairburn's side chick. But you screw with me and I *will* do it. Understand?"

Shivering, Paige nodded.

"Good. Now come in and sit down on the bed. I need to make a couple calls."

Dazed and numb, she obeyed. 415 pulled a chair to the edge of the hallway, blocking the one exit. Then he dialed a number, his gun still aimed directly at her.

"Mr. Vaughn? This is Novak. We have a situation. Turns out that Fairburn's screwing some of his cleaning staff. One of these air-heads spotted our collection and decided to take pictures. I caught her—what do you want me to do?"

The answer was short and quick—and she couldn't hear a word of it. "Will do. Thanks."

Heart pounding, Paige waited to hear her fate. Novak watched her, savoring the fear she couldn't hide. Just when she'd decided to jump out the window and take her chances with the four-story drop, he yawned. "Sit tight. My boss is sending a fixer to clean this mess up."

Wasn't 'fixer' another word for 'assassin'? At least in the movies, anyway. "What is he going to do?"

"Probably move our collection." A flash of irritation glittered in his eyes. "Keep yapping at me, though, and he'll have to dispose of a body too."

Okay. She could take a hint. Paige leaned back against the headboard and waited.

Ten minutes later, someone let themselves into the room. Novak stood to let a scrawny man slip past. Nothing about the newcomer caught the eye, not his thin, pinched lips, pock-marked face, or dull tan clothes. "That her phone on the floor back there?"

Novak nodded. He walked to the head of the bed, but, to her great relief, set his gun down on the tv before he came over. That relief only lasted a second. Quick as a rattlesnake, his hand lashed out and clamped across her mouth. With practiced ease, he pinned her to the bed and called out, "There's some cord in the closet. Grab that for me, would you?"

Frantically, Paige clawed at his arms, her nails digging red lines down his arm. Novak's eyes glittered, as if he enjoyed the struggle. "Hey, I wasn't lying when I said I didn't want to shoot you. Too much blood. Pisses the fixer off. Strangling's a lot neater."

The fixer wandered around the corner, her phone in his hand. "We aren't killing her."

Relief flooded her and her desperate struggle petered out. That news didn't please Novak, though. "Why the hell not?"

"Boss said not to. Though," his faded eyes met hers and Paige saw a glint of malice in them, "if she doesn't cooperate, I am authorized to change that. What's your phone's password, ma'am?"

Novak's grip didn't relent one bit and she felt her teeth cut into her own lip. "This is insane. Killing her is the easiest route."

"Boss has other plans and I don't sass him. Now, get your

hand off her mouth so she can tell me her password." The skinny man glanced back at her and added, "Scream, and I'll let him kill you. Understood?"

Paige nodded weakly. As Novak released her, she scrambled away. The coppery taste of blood filled her mouth.

"Password?"

"1218." *December 18th. Jake's birthday.*

The fixer typed it in and flipped through her apps. Novak began to pace back and forth like a caged wolf. "What are we doing?"

"I'm fixing things. You're sitting down and shutting up."

Denied an opportunity for murder, Novak retrieved his gun and sat, glaring at her. Paige waited and prayed.

After a couple minutes, the small man smiled. "Well, good. I think I can sort this out without killing anybody. Just like the boss wants."

Novak's eyes lit with outrage. "Why the hell does a worm give a shit about one stupid maid?"

'Worm.' Even in her fear, Paige noted that word. What a strange, contemptuous thing to call your boss!

The fixer didn't object to it. "Why don't you ask him?" he jeered. "Go on. Tell him he's wrong. Just let me know when you're gonna do it, though, because I want to watch him tear you to pieces."

The two men glowered at each other in open loathing. It sickened her to think of these monsters, these *villains*, working with Rex. Yet, impossible as it seemed, Paige couldn't dismiss the idea.

In the end, Novak turned away, spitting on the floor.

Smirking, the fixer addressed his words to her. "I'm leaving now. Probably take me an hour or two to straighten this out. You need to sit here, calm and quiet. If you do, you'll walk out unharmed, okay?" She nodded, trembling. His gaze hardened as he turned to Novak. "Your job is to keep her quiet—and alive. If she ends up dead while I'm gone, I've got permission to kill *you*."

Novak threw his head back and barked with laughter. "I'd like to see you try!"

"You wouldn't. 'Cause I'd do it from a quarter mile away, with a sniper rifle."

That wiped the grin off her captor's face. Though it didn't do much to settle Paige's nerves.

"Trust me," the fixer said. The guy with the oh-so-untrustworthy face. "Everybody stay calm and we all get to live long, happy lives. Sound good?"

Sounded good to her! Paige nodded. Novak scowled.

The next hour and a half were agony. Those ninety minutes ticked by at a glacial pace. Novak stalked about the room, snarling and muttering to himself. On every pass, she was sure he'd change his mind and kill her out of sheer frustration. Curled in a ball, Paige stayed as still as a mouse, watching the seconds and minutes crawl by.

Ages later, a soft click announced the return of the fixer. To her relief (and Novak's irritation), the small man smiled as he entered the room. "Done. You're free to go, Miss Hall."

"The hell she is!" Snarling with outrage, Novak bolted to his feet. "You can't seriously think we can just let her walk out of here."

"We can. And here's why." One look at his calm, narrow face warned her that the worst was still to come. "Miss Hall, I left your phone on your kitchen table."

On her... Wait. He'd gone to her house? Paige's eyes widened in horror.

The small man nodded. "You know where this is going. Your son Jake is no longer at your neighbor Judy's house."

'Common sense' and all thoughts of self-preservation flew from her mind. Paige scrambled to her feet and slapped the man as hard as she could. "Where is he?"

Novak burst out laughing. The fixer just scowled. "Some-place safe. Hit me again and that will change." Hands clenching and opening, she glared at him, torn between rage and despair. "Do you want to see your son again, Miss Hall?"

"Yes," she groaned, fighting tears.

"Then you need to get yourself under control. Your son's fate depends on your behavior. Sit down."

Shaking with rage, she sank to the bed.

"Thank you. Here's how you keep your boy safe. You walk out of this room and go straight home. If your supervisor calls, you blow her off. Say you're sick. Quit. I don't care. Just don't come back to this place for any reason."

This morning, losing her job seemed like a catastrophe. Now, she didn't care. She knew what real disaster looked like.

"In a week or two, when we're done here, I'll give you a call. If you've been cooperative, I'll give you the name of a rest area where you can go and pick your son up, safe and sound. No one will get hurt. You'll never see us again. End of story."

Novak shook his head in disgust. "I still don't get why we don't just throttle her and dump her body someplace."

"Because you're not in charge," the fixer murmured. His beady eyes never left her face. "One more thing, Miss Hall. It probably goes without saying, but I'm going to spell it out just in case: don't tell anyone about this. If you go to the police… if you whine to Mr. Fairburn… if you even berate your neighbor for not watching your son closely… you will never see your boy again. Understand?"

Oh, she understood. Novak didn't leave her any delusions about how terrible these people were.

Sick and shaking, Paige nodded.

CHAPTER 9

By the time Friday rolled around, Rex had come to hate Ancestral Puebloan ruins. He hated their cliff dwellings. He despised their kivas, both round and square. And he especially loathed the fact that they always built the damned things in the middle of nowhere on some godforsaken mesa you had to plod through five miles of badlands to reach.

He loved Rats, though. SueSue and her people were a gift from heaven. Every Shifter within three counties 'worried' about this new Fangs of Apophis threat. And every one of them would gladly sit down over beers and tell Rex exactly what they thought *he* ought to do about it. The Rats? Well, they were the only ones lifting a paw to help. Them and the First Flight folks. SueSue's Kind swept through the desert, peeking below cliffs and poking their noses into every dusty cranny. Nobody found another blob monster–but they returned with scores of pictures of beat up old ruins.

Having checked a couple sites himself, he knew how much work that took. And he was grateful.

He'd be *more* grateful if they'd turned up answers. But

none of the pictures revealed what the Fangs were up to. Five days later, the Witch Hares could guess where the Fangs might hit—but not why.

Finn and Bree Donnelly wanted to keep going. One of these sites 'had' to hold the proof they needed. Rex, he wasn't convinced. And while he puttered around out in the badlands, work piled up at his resorts. So, around noon, he begged off of another hike out to some godforsaken rock pile. While the Dragon and his Mate drove off in search of clues, he headed up to Ancient Ways, where a dozen silly 'emergencies' demanded his attention.

Three hours and one very relieved manager later, Rex decided to call it a day. Maybe there were demon-summoning lunatics in town, but a man still needed to relax. Toss back a couple of beers, shoot some pool, and he might feel human again. Though….

He glanced down the hall toward housekeeping. Beers went down better with company.

All week long he'd struggled to keep his mind on his work. That shouldn't have been hard. Alone in the desert, he *ought* to watch for any sludge monsters or Fangs lurking along the trail.

Instead, time and again, he found his thoughts drifting to her.

Paige. He worried about her, endlessly.

Monday afternoon was the worst. Halfway out to a ruin, a hunch hit him like a sledgehammer. Something was wrong at Ancient Ways. Paige was in danger! Saturday, with the sludge monster, was still fresh in his mind and so he ran five miles, before he could get bars on his phone. Cursing himself every step of the way for not getting her phone number.

Yet, when he finally managed to get Mrs. Gordon on the line, she assured him that all was well. Nothing amiss at

Ancient Ways. Paige was fine (though cleaning a particularly dirty room). Why, she'd just talked to her.

By then, he was embarrassed. Rex Fairburn was not a man who let vapors and moods and hunches run his life. He turned around and stomped all the way back to that ruin, feelings be damned. But no matter what he did, those ridiculous worries wouldn't leave him. With gritted teeth, he finished his job, hiked to the car... and then couldn't stop himself from driving past Paige's house.

She was there, sitting in the living room. Watching tv.

Not a sign of anything wrong.

He thought about checking in with her, but other memories stopped him. The softness of her body, warm and welcoming beneath him. The way she lit up with joy at his touch—and how the sadness that seemed to surround her vanished under the blaze of their passion.

No, better to keep his distance. He didn't trust himself to remember that he *couldn't* get in a relationship right now. One hook-up was a shame. Two in two days... well, that was just low. Paige deserved better.

The whole shitty week passed like that. For five days, he'd ghosted through his life, lost in worries, memories and dreams of her. The kids weren't any help, either. They babbled about her all the time and made an embarrassing fuss when their old sitter, Judy, showed up to watch them.

"Judy never does *anything* with us!" Micah groaned.

"She makes eggs raw!" Sam wailed.

They probably had a point. As far as Rex could see, Judy spent most of her time watching tv and fiddling with her phone. At least she was competent, though.

When she showed up.

Once more, Rex stared down toward Ancient Ways' housekeeping unit and rubbed his chin. Would Paige be willing to quit? He could hire her as his full-time....

Mate! his Bear suggested.

I'm not looking for a Mate, he reminded it.

A flood of images filled his mind, floating in a sea of long-ing. A Mate to sleep beside him. A mother to watch over his children. A Mate to fight beside him. Food when he came home to the Den. Someone for him to bring food back to. *More* kids!

That made him smile. Apparently, five small children wasn't enough for some creatures! Yet, in the midst of its foolish, Bear-ish yearning, one painful truth remained: he missed having a full family. He missed a woman's touch, the way she transformed a house into a home. Rex loved his chil-dren, both natural and adopted. But he couldn't deny that caring for them, raising them, took a toll on him. They deserved more. They deserved better.

They deserved a mother.

Mate!

"Yeah, yeah, whatever you want to call it."

Even as he admitted this, a cold void opened up in his heart. His children had already had mothers—and they died. All this talk about the Fangs of Apophis made him wonder if those deaths had truly been accidents... or something worse.

Could he drag Paige into that? Into a world of Shifters and magic and deadly conspiracies? Could he ask her to subject her own son to the risks his children were forced, by birth, to face?

Could he risk caring for her, knowing that she might well die?

No. That was too much. For her, *and* for him.

Beer? his Bear urged. *And her?*

Rex burst out laughing, then quickly choked it back before someone heard. "Think you're being clever, don't you?"

His Bear said nothing. 800 pounds of pure, honey-covered innocence.

Okay, he had to admit, it would be fun. And he wouldn't give in to temptation, because he knew where he stood. Where they *both* stood; Paige didn't want danger or a new relationship either. Besides, it was just a beer, right?

His Bear radiated approval.

Right. What the hell. Rex headed down the hall and knocked on Mrs. Gordon's open door.

"What?" she snapped. As soon as she recognized him, that querulous tone vanished. "Oh, Mr. Fairburn!" she simpered, quickly smoothing her dress. "I didn't know you were stopping by today!"

"Sorry to intrude. Is Paige Hall still here or has she gone home for the day?"

The older woman sighed with loud, dramatic sorrow. "I'm afraid she didn't come in today."

All of the week's fears rushed back and with a bone-rattling snarl, his Bear came awake. Rex tried to calm it; there were plenty of reasons for missing work. "Is she sick?"

"I don't know. She didn't really say."

"You're her supervisor." The edge of his Bear's rage turned those words into a growl. "Surely, you don't let cleaners come and go without explanation? What's going on?"

Faced with that anger, the supervisor wilted. "Well, it's… it's not really my place to say, but…."

His Bear's agitation grew, and with it came an intense urge to start batting all the furniture over. Rex gritted his teeth and tried to ignore the angry creature. "Tell me. Now."

Mrs. Gordon's nervousness collapsed into a sulky, bitter pout. "Paige Hall completely changed after… well, after this weekend."

After they made love. He scowled at the implication.

"Suddenly, she was too good to clean messy rooms! Yelled at me, too, about how she'd talk to you if I didn't do what she said. I told her to go back and do her work, but she walked off in a huff. I had to send someone else to finish her work after the room complained."

That didn't sound right! Paige had been very clear about how much she needed this job....

Until he gave her a couple thousand dollars.

The first tendrils of doubt crept into his thoughts. His Bear wasn't having any of this, but Rex couldn't force that dark question from his mind.

"Next morning, she wasn't here. No call. No excuses. I phoned her myself, of course, and she just said she had no plans to come to work. Maybe for a couple weeks."

Enough time to spend the cash he gave her?

"As if I'm going to keep a job open for her that long! Unless you want me to, of course." Mrs. Gordon cringed and glanced up at him. "She seemed to think that because of your... because she knew you, she could do that."

"She most certainly cannot," Rex seethed. "You're in charge of housekeeping. Staffing is your decision and I'll respect that."

The woman melted into a gloating simper. Lost in his anger, Rex barely noticed. How *dare* Paige take advantage of his generosity? How dare she presume that a brief hook-up....

DO NOT INSULT OUR MATE! his Bear roared. Rex ignored it too.

...gave her special privileges at work?

"Don't worry, Mrs. Gordon. I'll speak to Miss Hall and tell her she needn't return to Ancient Ways."

"Thank you so much for taking care of this, Mr. Fairburn! Thank you!"

He stalked out of the office, buffeted by two contradictory rages. His anger with Paige. His Bear's fury with him.

Something bobbed in the midst of that sea of anger. One small fact, something…forgotten. Rex paused, baffled by that sense that he was forgetting something. Something obvious, and important.

Damned if he knew what it was, though—and he wasn't a man who worried about whims and hunches.

Shaking his head, he stormed off to confront his reprobate lover.

HE HAD TO POUND ON THE DOOR FOR A FULL MINUTE BEFORE Paige answered. The first sight of her face—ashen, drawn, hostile—kicked the feet out from under his 'righteous' outrage.

"What do you want?" The screen door stayed closed.

"We need to talk." He tried to summon back his indignation, while his Bear snuffled wildly, sure something was wrong.

She just stood there. Silent, staring into the distance until he was sure he'd need to push his way in. Then, with a sigh, she unlatched the hook. "Whatever."

What the hell had happened? Rex followed her to the living room, noting the house's complete silence. Curtains covered all the windows, filling its rooms with a cool dimness. Dirty dishes littered the coffee table. The only light came from the television. Volume off, it played silent infomercials, endlessly.

Paige collapsed on the couch. "What do you want?"

Uneasy, he circled around the chair rather than taking a seat. "I want to know why you haven't been at work this week."

"Your *partners*," she spat the word, a helpless rage filling her eyes with tears, "told me to stay home."

Partners? Did she mean the Donnellys? Or Mrs. Gordon? "What are you talking about?"

The tears welled higher, threatening to spill down her cheeks. "Is this a test? I know I'm not supposed to 'whine' to you."

None of this made sense. His agitated Bear shifted from foot to foot, grumbling. "Did Mrs. Gordon forbid you from speaking to me?"

Now, the first tear did break free, tracing a glittering trail down her face. "Go away. I won't talk. I'll pass your damn test," she hissed.

"What test? What do you mean?"

She didn't answer. Shivering, she tucked her knees under her chin and wrapped her arms around them, a ball of pure, undistilled misery. Rex longed to pull her close. To force her, with kisses and the heat of his touch, to trust him and confide in him. But she'd made it clear that the passion they'd shared was gone. Long gone.

The quiet weighed on him. It drove his Bear crazy and Rex found himself shifting from foot to foot, waiting for an explanation. The creak of the boards beneath his feet was the only sound to break the stillness.

And suddenly, he realized why that fact was so ominous. "Where's Jake?"

Paige screamed, a wail of grief that froze him in his tracks. "Screw you!" she howled, over and over again, as she dissolved in tears.

Bear and man acted as one, united in their love for her. Rex bolted to the couch and swept her into his arms. Weeping, she pounded on his chest, pouring her pain into those blows. Silent, stoic, he let her pour her feelings out until, rage spent, she collapsed against him. As sobs shook her body, he held her, gently stroking her hair. In the end, even grief failed her. Paige grew still as despair killed her sobs.

And when she was quiet, he was still there. Waiting patiently.

"Tell me what happened," he begged her.

"I can't." Her tear-stained face turned up to him, brown eyes accusing. "If you're not working with them, why didn't you come when I called?"

"You called? When?"

"Monday. From work."

Wait. Monday…?

Nausea twisted his guts and his Bear keened, a howl of shame and horror. Something *had* happened that day. Something that he, in his pride, had ignored.

He'd failed this woman. Badly.

Our Mate. This time, Rex didn't even have the strength to correct his grieving Bear. *We didn't protect our Mate.*

"I didn't get your call," he whispered.

"Mrs. Gordon spoke to you…didn't she?" When he shook his head, anger lit her eyes. A welcome change from the grey despair that had choked her. "Then she lied. She said you thought I was stupid to worry."

"About what?"

"I can't tell you. Jake's life depends on it. Please, you have to trust me!"

"I do trust you. It's *them* I worry about. Paige, listen to me." Rex dropped to his knees in front of her, holding her hands. "If Jake is in danger, you need to tell me what happened. I will save him, I promise. I screwed up on Monday, but I swear that I will protect both of you."

"They said I'd never see him again if I 'whined' to you," she said in a stricken whisper.

Wrapped in the power of his Bear's will, his voice vibrated with confidence. "What makes you think they'll let

Jake go even if you do what they say? Paige, you need to make a decision: what do you trust more? Their threats—or my word?"

Fear and love warred in her face. A mother's terror for her son. The hope, faint but intense, that there was someone in this world she could lean on. A friend, a protector... yes, a lover who could shield her from the world's evil.

In the end, love won. "I trust *you*," she whispered.

Then the truth came out. The deadly standoff in Room 415. Mrs. Gordon's lies (Rex made a note to fire that damned harpy as soon as life calmed down for five minutes). Jake, and the men who kidnapped him.

"Were they Shifters?"

"How could I tell? I mean, nobody Shifted."

As a Shifter himself, he'd know just by looking at them. And yes, there had been some Shifters at Ancient Ways this summer. Not unusual, since it was the nicest resort in the area. For a human, though, it was a tough question. "Did they say or do anything unusual?"

"Like, um, kidnapping my son?"

"Ugh. I mean, 'normal' for a human criminal. Our Spirit Animals often echo in our human form. Like me. I'm a Bear. Bears are all big guys and ladies. Wolves lose their shit if they get locked up in a small room."

At that, she straightened. "Novak didn't handle the wait well. He kept pacing back and forth across the room."

Good! That was a clue. "Maybe a Wolf then. No women, so probably no Hares. You said the fixer was a small man with a skinny face. When you saw him, did you get any hunches or feelings?"

"I knew he was bad news. No matter how polite he was, there was something about him. Something...."

She hesitated, at a loss for words. "Untrustworthy?" Rex suggested.

"Yes! Exactly!"

"That's common for Rats." It took a long time to get used to that poor Kind. "Okay, so we've got a Wolf and a Rat. You probably didn't get a chance to learn anything about their boss."

"No, I… hang on! They did say something weird. Novak insulted him. He called him a 'worm' and the fixer didn't give him grief for that."

A Worm. Rex felt his stomach drop at the word. He was a Bear, fierce and strong. No enemy ever made him back down. But Worms were as bad as it got.

Paige spotted his doubt in a heartbeat. "What is it? What's wrong?"

Should he lie? Protect her from the terrible truth?

No, that kind of 'protection' crippled your Mate.

Damn you, Bear! Now you've got me *saying it!*

"You remember Finn Donnelly?"

"Yes. I'm not forgetting the first time I saw a Dragon."

"Well, when a Dragon gives in to evil, their Spirit Animal tears itself apart. Claws its own wings off. Once that happens, we don't call them 'Dragons' anymore. We call them…."

"Worms." She understood what that meant for her son. He could see it in her stricken, ashen face.

"I don't know why a Worm would spare you. That's the only detail that doesn't make sense to me. But, well, I think we've got a huge problem. These guys have to be working for the Fangs of Apophis, the gang Donnelly told us about."

Her shoulders slumped as despair returned. The sight of it roused his Bear into a red-hot, protective anger. "What can we do?"

He needed help. But who?

Donnelly seemed like the obvious choice—and the only Shifter in the state who would stand a chance going toe-to-

toe with a Worm. But he was as subtle as a freight train. If they had to fight, they had already lost. Jake would be dead or gone.

And he couldn't do that to Paige. Saving her son was the first order of business. Kicking the Fangs' asses would have to wait.

"I'm going to ask for a bit of help."

"No!" She sprang to her feet, eyes widening. "If we tell everyone, they'll find out! They…!"

"Paige, hush." Once more, he took her hands, wrapping them in the warmth of his own broad mitts. "It's just going to be one or two people. Shifters I know can keep a secret. Trust me, okay?"

A weak nod was his only answer.

Now, he needed to make sure he didn't betray her trust.

CHAPTER 10

*N*othing about Lily King said 'subtle' or 'discreet.'

The strange woman stalked into Paige's living room and peeled off her helmet to reveal a delicate, fine-boned face—the face of an angel. Nothing else about her was angelic, though. Black pants and jacket made from some strange, form-fitting mesh fabric. Leather boots and gloves. And mud. Tons of mud. Spattered across everything and dried to a rock.

Rex offered her a hand. "Lily. Thanks for coming."

"You owe me, Big Man. What's up?"

He quickly filled her in on the situation. Jake's abduction, the strange Shifters. "I think these may be those Fangs of Apophis that the First Flight warned about."

An eager light bloomed in her green eyes. "We attacking? You want me to summon the Pack?"

Pack? Lily must be a Wolf then. Paige studied her, curious. The only other Shifter women she'd seen were Hares, delicate and beautiful. Lily was gorgeous too. But a wildness, a hint of danger, lurked behind those wide green eyes.

This was *not* a woman she wanted to cross. Or, honestly, have much to do with.

But Rex thought they needed her help. "I need to rescue Jake first. Can't risk hurting him. To do that, I need to know who his kidnapper is. Can you check the neighbor's yard for any clues? I smelled something over there. I think it's a Rat, but I'm not sure."

"You're not sure?" Lily broke into a grin that revealed a *lot* of white teeth. "Damn, Smokey, you need to work on your tracking. Nose like yours, you ought to rock."

"Yeah, yeah. Can you do this for me?"

"Sure." Paige froze as Lily turned toward her. The Wolf's eyes raked over her once then dismissed her, like a field mouse. "She Kin?"

"No," her lover replied as she blushed. "Though she's seen Shifts. She'll be fine."

"Okaaay."

The doubt in the Wolf's tone made Paige grit her teeth. She was *not* going to flip out, no matter what happened!

In fact, it wasn't scary at all. A silvery aura shimmered across Lili's body, filling the room with its pale glow. When it faded, a she-wolf stood in front of the couch. Tall, long-legged and proud, with a thick brown coat tipped with black. A collar circled her throat, decorated with a strange silver medallion. The pattern of wavy lines on it looked vaguely familiar, like something from a Hopi pot.

She was beautiful. Paige felt a pang of jealousy.

Frowning, Rex opened the door for her. No more than three minutes later, she trotted back and Shifted into her human form.

"Yep. Rat. Took the kid. Bit of a struggle. I'm guessing the Rat used chloroform or something on him."

Paige inhaled sharply at that.

"He put the kid's body in his Jeep and took off. Don't know where he's keeping the boy. Maybe off-road, but not too far."

"How could you possibly know that stuff?" Paige protested. "The type of car? Where they were going?"

The Wolf's head snapped toward her. Burning eyes locked with hers and, after a second of shock, Paige glanced away.

Establishing dominance. That's what Wolves did, right?

Having made her point, Lily relented. "I *know* that, woman, because of its tires. They're not the junk you pick up at Walmart. Deep tread for gripping rocks. Your Rat expects to be driving across sand and gravel—not on roads. But for off-road, those tires should be slightly deflated, and they're not. That means, either he's careful—he deflates his tires only when necessary. Or he's not heading into the wilderness."

Rex gave her elbow an apologetic squeeze. "Lily's good at this stuff. That's why I asked her to help." He glanced back at the Wolf, studying her with an intensity that roused a flash of foolish jealousy in Paige's heart. "By the way, what's up with the necklace? I've never seen an item that didn't vanish during a Shift."

Necklace? Oh, the 'collar.' On second thought, Paige was *really* glad she hadn't called it that.

Lily shrugged his question off. "No idea. It started doing that recently. I'm guessing it's magic."

"You ought to take it to a Hare. Figure out why that happens."

The Wolf's nose wrinkled. "There's only one thing rabbits are good for, and it's not pawing over my stuff."

"Well, *I* would take it to a Hare," the Bear grumbled, "but you be you. Thank you for your help, Lily. It means a lot to me."

Paige was less enthusiastic. They'd gotten information,

yes—though nothing that got them any closer to finding her son. "What do we do now?"

"Now, we go talk to SueSue Mint. She's the matriarch of the Rats in this area. If you can describe this guy, she may know him or where he's hiding."

"Or I could just follow him," Lily offered.

She and Rex both stared in shock at the Wolf. "You can track cars? On roads?" the Bear asked.

"Yeah."

"Five-day-old tracks?"

"Yeah."

"Since when?"

"Since a couple years ago."

Rex grew thoughtful. "About the time that the Wellsprings supposedly woke up."

"Yep. Which is why I didn't laugh the First Flight out of the room when they said that."

Once more, his eyes trailed back to that necklace. "Can all Wolves do this or just you?"

"Just me. We going to find this kid, or do you want to grab a couple beers and shoot the shit?"

This time, Paige agreed with the Wolf. None of this stuff got her any closer to Jake.

"Good point. I'll follow you in the Jeep." Wincing, her lover drew her close and kissed her gently on the forehead. "We'll be back as soon as we can. And I promise you, we'll save Jake."

"Shouldn't I come?"

"No. If Lily can track this Rat directly, we're walking straight into danger."

Lily rolled her eyes. "Yeah, no reason for you to come— unless you like your kid. Or want him back for some other reason."

"Lily!" Rex growled.

The Wolf wasn't the least bit intimidated by his furious glare. "What?"

"Paige isn't a Shifter."

"She's a mother, isn't she? This is *her* kid? Then maybe she wants to help save his ass."

She did, with every ounce of her heart. It sickened her to think of sitting here, alone in the gloom, watching the minutes tick by and praying that someone else would save the most precious thing in her world.

"This is too dangerous!" Rex thundered. Paige could imagine his grizzly, standing on its hind legs and bellowing.

And still, the Wolf didn't back down. "The Pack hunts together. *All* of it."

"Dammit, she's not a Wolf!"

Ignoring him, Lily turned to her. All mocking, all contempt, had vanished from her heart-shaped face. "Do you want to help save your son?"

"I–"

"No! Out of the question! I forbid it!" Rex roared.

"You don't get to 'forbid' anything, Fairburn!" Lily snarled back. Dwarfed by the huge man, she was still a ball of furious rebellion. "It's *her* choice!"

"She can't do anything!"

Like a slap in the face, his words knocked the wind out of Paige. Tears welled up in her eyes as she realized he was right. She was useless. Weak. A babysitter and a maid. She'd just get in the way.

Lily didn't agree, though. "Then she's the Omega Wolf. No big deal. Every Pack has one. Dumbass loner Bear like you wouldn't know it, but I've been saved by Omegas a dozen times." Before he could protest, she whirled back to Paige. "So, what do you say? Do you want to help save your son?"

"I… He's right." Shame set her cheeks on fire. "I don't know what I could do."

"Do you want to find out?" Proud and defiant, the Wolf faced her. Something in her posture—the proud tilt of her head, the defiant cast of her shoulders—lit a tiny flame inside of Paige's heart. "Weakness is a choice. Every day, you choose not to find your strength. Today could be the day you stop."

"I…." Rex was angrily shaking his head and some cowardly corner of her mind wanted to crawl under the bed. To let a man or this strong woman defend her son. But Lily was right. She was a mother. Protecting Jake was *her* job too. How could she live with herself if she abandoned him? "Yes. I want that."

"Good. Then it's settled. You're coming."

"No!" Rex yelled.

"Yes!" Paige was glad that the Wolf, not her, had to face his anger. "Remember your question? Yeah, I'm the only Wolf who can track like this. And I don't go without her. Either you let her help find her kid—or you do this on your own. I won't lock her out."

As Rex hesitated, wrestling with that conundrum, Lily stalked toward the front door. "C'mon Puppy-Girl. Let's get you a weapon."

Paige almost tiptoed past the irate Bear and hustled to catch up with the Wolf. "I've never shot a gun," she admitted.

"Which is why I'm not giving you one today. You'd be more likely to shoot yourself—or me!—than the Bad Guys." A mud-spattered backpack was strapped to the back of her dirt bike. Lily rummaged through it. "By the way, if you want to change that, talk to me later on. I can teach you to shoot. Your boy too."

"Jake's only seven!"

"I was five when my father taught me."

Wolves clearly raised their kids differently than people!

Paige glanced back at the doorway where Rex stood glowering with disapproval.

"Here we go. Hunting knife… strap that thing on, Puppy-Girl…."

The knife was enormous. Dutifully, she looped the belt around her waist and tightened it, even as doubts gnawed at her. Could she really stab someone?

To save Jake? Yeah, I could.

I think… maybe….

"…and there we go! Combat flashlight."

Combat…what? With a flash of outrage, she realized that the Shifter woman had been teasing her all along. "Oh, har har! Puppy-Girl gets a flashlight. Nice one."

With a gleam in her eye, Lily yanked a long black baton out of her backpack. Before Paige could ask what it was, the Wolf pointed it at her face.

The world exploded into light. Blinded, she cringed—and then a hard, metallic bar rapped her on the head hard enough to make her yelp.

"Combat flashlight," Lily repeated. "This end blinds up to about twenty feet." The light vanished, leaving a sea of black dots floating before Paige's eyes. "Flip it around and it doubles as a club."

Lily held it out. Paige accepted it gingerly as she fought to blink the dots away. She turned it in her hands, shocked by its solid, heavy bulk. "Okay, I think I love this thing." Blinding people seemed much more do-able than stabbing them. Less blood.

"Keep it! It's yours."

"Oh, I couldn't take your flashlight!"

"No worries. I got a dozen of 'em," the Wolf assured her. "And every girl ought to have one."

Paige glanced between the two Shifters, so different. Rex,

a solid mountain of raw disapproval. Lily, small and mean and ready to fight.

Together, they could save her son. Bear, Wolf, and, uh… Puppy-Girl.

She forced herself to give them a smile (though it was nowhere near as dangerous as Lily's). "Let's go then!"

CHAPTER 11

*L*ily was a furry bullet streaking along the edge of the road. Knuckles white around the steering wheel, Rex followed her—and fought the urge to run her over.

Damned meddling idiotic fool of a Wolf!

His Bear shared his anger, roaring and swatting angrily at nothing. The two of them stewed, filling the Jeep with a furious silence.

Still as a mouse, Paige endured his anger, clutching her flashlight like a magic charm. Her *flashlight*.

Once more, he sent venomous thoughts winging toward the Wolf. His….

MATE! howled his Bear.

…babysitter was walking into a fight, armed with nothing more than a flashlight and a knife he doubted she dared to use. If Paige got hurt today, he was going to tear Lily apart.

He expected their quarry to head straight into Cortez. Instead, Lily circled east, taking backroads and trails that meandered toward Mesa Verde. Rex cruised after her at a steady 15mph. Helluva speed to run. Slow as molasses in a Jeep.

"I had to do this." Soft as a summer breeze, Paige's voice finally broke the tense stillness.

"No, you didn't. Lily's an idiot and she talked you into it. Look, don't be stupid. I can let you out here and pick you up on the way back."

"No. I want to help save Jake."

"Well that's not what's going to happen." Fear added a harsh edge to his words, and he winced to see her flinch. So did his Bear.

Do not swat our Mate.

Could this thing *not* stop calling her that? "Now I've got to save your son *and* worry about you at the same time. You've just made this job twice as hard."

"You don't need to worry about me." She had a chokehold on that ridiculous flashlight. "Just save Jake."

"I don't need to worry? Ha!" She cringed at his bark of laughter, winning a moan of displeasure from his Bear. "Have you ever been in combat? No? Then hell yeah, I have to worry!"

"Why?"

"Because you'll get killed!"

With no warning, Paige spun to face him and screamed at the top of her lungs. "So what?"

Unexpected, that howl of pain sent his Bear backpedaling furiously. As startled as if its Mate had suddenly transformed into a rabid wolverine.

Big wimp, Rex snarled at it. His Bear rose to its hind legs and continued inching away, staring anxiously at the infuriated woman.

Rex, however, was made of sterner stuff. In a calmer voice, he said, "It matters if you get hurt."

"Only to Jake."

"To me too."

Meant to soothe her, his soft words had the opposite

effect. "Right. Because if I got killed, you'd have to find another babysitter. No, wait!" Her laughter, bitter and hysterical, shocked him. "Scratch that. You've got Judy. I'm just the backup babysitter. And trust me, Mrs. Gordon has already found a replacement at Ancient Ways, so you won't be inconvenienced there, either."

Ahead of them, Lily paused, panting. Rex drifted to the side of the road and parked, still stunned by Paige's accusation. "Is that what you think you are to me? A babysitter?"

"Secondary babysitter." She glared straight ahead, throttling the flashlight.

"After everything we shared—"

"Stop! Stop it, right now!" Finally, one hand abandoned its death grip on her light—but only to jab an accusing finger in his face. "You made it very clear that you think what we shared was nothing. A hook up. A fling. A one-night stand."

"That's not true!"

"*You* said you weren't interested in a relationship! So, if we're not in a relationship and I'm not your employee, what *am* I to you?"

"You're a… a friend!"

"Bullshit! Friends do things together. We don't. And I don't want to be your 'friend' anyway!"

An anxious keening wove through his thoughts. Rex had never seen his Bear this upset before. He closed his eyes and pinched the bridge of his nose, trying to fight the beginning of a monstrous headache.

"And another thing!" Paige began.

He held up a hand weakly. "Hang on. Just give me a second. I have to… ugh."

Like a light switching off, her anger evaporated. "What's wrong?" She leaned close, scanning his face anxiously.

"It's nothing. Just my Bear."

"Does it sense something? Is there something wrong?"

"No, it's upset that we're arguing." He gave her a helpless shrug. "Keeps screaming 'MAKE THE MATE HAPPY!' I think my head's going to burst."

For a second, she stared at him, disbelieving. Then her lip twitched once… twice… and she burst into laughter. Not the harsh brays that shook her before. This was a real laugh, kind and gentle.

Even he had to smile, and his Bear snuffled, pleased by this sudden and confusing change. "Sorry. Bears are simple creatures."

He sat, listening to her laughter, letting it wash away the fight's terrible adrenaline. At last, she quieted. This time, the silence wasn't full of knives and bitterness.

"What's a 'Mate'?"

He glanced at his side view mirror, unwilling to meet her gaze. "About what you'd think. A wife. A soulmate. A mother Bear to guard your Den with you."

"Doesn't your Bear know I'm not a Shifter?"

"It does. Shifters don't just Mate with their own Kind. Shifter, Kin, mortal woman… it doesn't matter. From day one, my Bear had you pegged as my Mate."

"But you don't agree."

Now she stared out her window too. Rex sighed. "Paige, I can't take another Mate."

"Why?" Finally, their eyes met. Tears brightened hers, begging him for the truth.

A plea he could not refuse. "Have you ever lost someone? I did. My wife Ashley… my Mate… died in a car accident four years ago. And if you haven't lost someone…." He swallowed hard as the memories bubbled back. "I can't explain it. I can't tell you how it feels to have the heart ripped out of your world. To wake up in the morning and realize that the most important part of your life is gone. And not just once. Every day you wake up, and you remember that. Again and again. It never ends. The world is shit and leftovers, and you're still stuck in it.

"You know what the worst part is?" Unnoticed, his hands balled into fists. "I don't think it was an accident anymore. Finding out about the Fangs, the Shifters they've murdered and kidnapped… it makes me wonder about Ashley. The Longs too. Sam and Nate's parents. They were Bears, like me. You can kill us with a gun—but it takes a damned big one. One that would bring down a grizzly. So, how did some crazy hitchhiker manage to murder two Bears?"

A soft touch drew him out of those bitter thoughts. Paige's hand lay on his, a gentle, calming warmth. "I'm sorry," she whispered.

That kindness was a balm for his soul. At long last, his Bear settled, dropping to all four. "I know I pissed you off when I said you couldn't come. Maybe it's not my place to tell you that, but I couldn't help it. Paige, I can't do this. I can't risk losing you, or… or…."

"Or caring again?"

He couldn't answer that. Wouldn't.

"Do you know why I had to come?" she asked.

"Jake. He's your son. Trust me, I get it. Nothing's more important to a Bear than his family."

"No, I could have let you save Jake. I trust you." She patted his hand, a vote of confidence that made his heart ache. "I had to come because Lily's right: I've been afraid all of my life."

Now it was her turn to struggle for words. "I stayed with Leonard for years because I was afraid of being alone. I didn't set boundaries; didn't insist he treat me right. No matter how much he drank, no matter what cruel thing he said, I stayed. I didn't find my spine at all until the night he cheated on me."

A low, threatening growl shook his Bear. Rex promised

himself that, if he survived tonight, he would find this 'Leonard' and teach him a lesson.

"Even then, I was a coward. Lily would have knifed Leonard for doing that. Me, I took Jake and ran. Left behind most of our clothes... a lot of money... I just got out."

"It's okay."

Paige shook her head. "No, it's not. I want to stop running. I *need* to. That's why I came."

He longed to deny that. To promise that she didn't need to face these dangers. *He* would protect her. *He* would guard her, and her son. And yet....

Would any Momma Bear accept such an offer? What Bear could leave her Cub's fate in the hands of another? A mother Bear was no delicate flower, no helpless creature to be locked away and sheltered. She was strong and powerful in her own right. A pillar of maternal love.

Could he ask Paige to be anything less, even if she wasn't a Shifter?

"Do you understand now?" she begged him.

Slowly, reluctantly, he nodded. "I think I do."

"Good." She leaned close, eyes boring deep into his soul. "Because you need to do the same thing. You need to stop running."

Shocked by that order, he leaned back. "Uh, I'm not running away from anything."

"Yes, you are. You said it yourself. You 'can't' commit... you 'can't' risk...." Her eyes were two pools of moonlight, glittering and magical. "You 'can't' love again. That's running, and you have to stop."

Bile burned in his throat. "Paige, you don't understand...."

"Yes, I do. I've ran all my life. I know exactly how scary it is to stop and face those fears. But you have to. For your children. For yourself. For...." She swallowed, a tremor passing along the delicate curve of her throat. "For me. Because I love you."

Those words hit him like a hammer's blow. To have his courage doubted… yet, could he deny it? Was his fear truly different from the terrors that afflicted other men?

Twined with that guilt, though, was a thread of joy. Paige loved him. *Him.* Despite the way he'd treated her. His Bear thrummed with contentment, radiating a faith that the world was the way it should be.

If he accepted her love.

If he said he loved her as well.

"Paige, I…."

With a loud thud, something slammed onto the hood of his Jeep. Paige shrieked, Rex whirled….

And found an annoyed Wolf staring through the windshield at them.

"Dammit, Lily!" He honked the horn.

Yelping, the Wolf shot straight into the air. Lights blazed around it and an indignant woman landed on the hood. "What the hell, Fairburn? You guys are supposed to be following me!"

"You stopped!" To his annoyance, Paige dropped his hand and went back to strangling her flashlight.

"Five minutes ago! Are we going to get this kid or what?"

"Of course!" he snapped. Painfully aware that some cowardly corner of his mind felt it had been saved by the bell.

Lily snorted and Shifted back to her Wolf form, then trotted down the road. He put the Jeep into gear and followed her.

Letting silence fill the car once more.

CHAPTER 12

*L*ost in her own thoughts, Paige almost missed the sign. Over and over again, their conversation ran on a constant replay loop in her mind. Each repetition raised new questions. What had Rex meant to say? What did the purse of his lips mean when she said she loved him? Was his voice warmer or cooler afterward?

Did he share her feelings?

Or had she made a fool of herself?

When Rex slammed on the brakes, she was jerked violently out of that reverie. Thank goodness for her seatbelt, which caught her as she pitched forward. The flashlight wasn't as lucky. It tumbled from her fingers and rolled across the floor.

What had happened? Anxiously, she scanned the scene ahead. Nothing stood out. A handful of beat up ranches and single-wide trailers lay ahead. Cars and rusting trucks littered their 'lawns' and lounged along the side of the road. No sign of Lily—until a stealthy movement in the drainage ditch caught Paige's eye. The Wolf had abandoned the road and now scurried along the ditch, belly to the ground.

She'd seen something. Something dangerous.

Lips growing suddenly dry, Paige stared at those dusty, ramshackle buildings. Jake was in one of them.

And his kidnappers.

"Open your door," Rex ordered. She did. Lily immediately hopped into her lap and bounded into the backseat. Calmly, looking neither left nor right, the Bear drove on.

"Blue house," Lily said. "The one with the Ford parked on the street."

He never even glanced at it. "Thoughts on best viewing?"

"Dryer's Road. The hill right before State Road 7."

As if nothing had happened, Rex drove on. At the next intersection, he turned left and cut a slow, leisurely curve around the house. A few miles later, at the crest of a small hill, he pulled over behind a small copse of junipers. "Now comes the boring part, for you," he told Paige as he grabbed a pair of binoculars out of the back. "Sit tight."

Time passed. *Again.* Scowling up at the blistering sun, she simmered with annoyance. How long had she waited this week? How much time had she spent sitting in agony, hoping things would get better?

No more. From now on, she was going to *do* things. She'd find her strength, like Lily said.

A brave resolution. Yet, she still doubted herself.

So, I'll be the hero next time. But not this time because... why? I got told to sit in the car?

Fortunately, the Shifters' return interrupted those dark thoughts, and Rex's first words snapped her completely out of her funk. "I think we can do this. Lily? Your plan, you explain it."

"Here's how it goes, Puppy-Girl." The Wolf poked her head between the front seats and spoke to Paige directly, ignoring the Bear. Like the two of them were the only ones here who mattered. "Single story ranch with a cellar door in the back. Three Wolves watching tv in the front room, no sign of anyone else upstairs. That means your boy's probably in the basement."

Paige clutched her flashlight and nodded.

"Land next door is covered with junipers. Rex drops you and me off out of sight. We approach under tree cover. Short dash—maybe a hundred feet—to the edge of the house. Stay close and keep low under the windows. We circle to the back and go in the cellar. Get your boy, get out… then Rex and I kick some ass while you move Jake to safety."

Simple and sensible. But….

"What if there's someone down there watching him? What if we get caught?"

"Then I howl my ass off and your Bear busts through the front door. If it comes to a fight, your job is to get your kid out. Got it? Leave the brawling to Rex and me. Get your kid. Get out."

"Understood."

Rex's teeth were clenched, and he glowered straight ahead. She longed to hug him, to promise that this would all turn out okay. But, well, it might not. Empty promises were useless. And he didn't seem like the kind of guy who wanted public displays of affection. At least not in front of the impish Wolf.

"Let's do this," he grumbled. Once more, the Jeep rolled forward. Left and left again, finishing the broad circle around the Fangs' lair. Just before it came into view, he pulled over. Lily scrambled out at once and Shifted into her smaller, Wolf form. As Paige began to follow her, Rex caught her hand.

Anguish filled his brown eyes and his lips were pinched with worry. Yet all he said was, "Be careful."

"I will." Lily waited, hackles rising at the delay. Paige slipped out and followed her before she grew too impatient.

The first part was simple. They jogged through the thin woods, hidden from view. With the Wolf's guidance, they came out at the rear of the house, away from most windows. One short, heart-pounding dash brought them to the cellar door.

Which was locked with a brand-new, enormous padlock.

As Paige's eyes widened in dismay, Lily Shifted back and produced a set of lock picks.

Of course. Trust the Wolf to be prepared for everything. Doubt cast a shadow over Paige, and her grip on her flashlight tightened. Why was she even here? She was dead weight.

The cellar door opened onto a short flight of steps with a second, normal door at the bottom. Lily crept down and pressed her face to the floor, staring at the crack. When she rose, she pointed at it and mouthed, 'Light.'

Jake? Or his captors? Mouth dry, Paige turned her flashlight on low, letting a tiny beam light the second lock. Lily nodded her approval, but the gesture did little to reassure her.

Look at me, I get to shine a light. If I do it well, maybe I'll be promoted, and they'll let me hold their coffee on the way home!

Sternly, she forced herself to focus. Self-doubt would just cripple her.

As if I'm not crippled enough already. Puppy-Girl, indeed.

Lily drew a small gun from somewhere under her vest, a sight that was both encouraging *and* humiliating. Carrying a gun was yet another thing no one trusted *her* to do. The Wolf opened the door and slipped through. When the room didn't immediately explode in gunfire, Paige joined her.

They stepped into a bare, basic cellar. Low ceiling, no more than six feet tall, dirt floor and cobwebs. A staircase rose in the center, leading up into the house. Along the far wall lay a cot and a sleeping bag. A heavy dog chain dangled from the beam over it, running down to the ankle of a small form.

Jake! A tidal wave of relief swept over her, making the world spin.

With no thought for her own safety, Paige dashed to her son's side. At her touch, he stirred. A tiny face, pinched with fear, peeked up at her. A fear that transformed to joy when he realized who she was washed over his features.

"Mommy!"

"Shush, baby," she whispered. "We're going to get you out of here."

With a grimace, Lily studied the chain holding her son. Paige simply pulled him close, wrapping him in her love and her arms. Promising, silently, that everything would be okay.

Upstairs, a floorboard creaked. She glanced at her partner, but the Wolf stood unmoving.

More creaks. Were those footsteps, coming closer? Jake trembled against her, shivers wracking his small body. Paige glared at the Wolf. What was she waiting for? She'd torn through the other lock in seconds! How hard could this one be?

But as her irritation grew, details suddenly chilled her. Lily's vacant stare. Her hands, dangling useless at her side. The way her mouth drooped, slightly open.

Fear brushed annoyance aside. Heart pounding, Paige looked up at the ceiling.

A plaque had been nailed to the beam, near the padlock that bound the chain. Black clay, about the size of a dinner plate. No decoration or writing—except for a spiral of white paint that curled into its center. It was about as dull as plates got… yet there was something freakishly compelling about it. Paige followed its spiraling path a couple of times before she realized she was wasting time.

Beneath it, the Shifter woman stood, still as a stone.

"Lily!" Paige caught her by the chin and forced her head down, away from the tantalizing line of that disk.

Eyes glazed and puzzled, Lily stared at her.

"Are you okay?" she whispered, terrified that someone would hear. At least the creaks had stopped. That was a good sign.

Right?

As soon as she let go of the woman's chin, the Wolf tilted her head back and continued her rapt study of the plate.

Paige's mouth grew dry. Was this… magic?

She still found it hard to believe—yet, was magic any stranger than Shifters?

Yeah, but what 'spell' would be strong enough to trap Lily and not me?

One that only targeted Shifters? A quick glance at Jake assured her that her son was no more dazzled than her. He watched her, pale eyes wide….

…and flickering to the stairs behind her.

With a gasp, Paige spun.

A woman stood at the base of the stairs. Slender, pale, she had the same strange blue-green eyes of Bree Donnelly and Danielle LePierre.

Hare, Paige realized. *Witch.*

The stranger raised a pistol and aimed it at Lily King.

Gun! her dazed brain observed.

Yet, even as her terrified mind chittered these useless, obvious facts, Paige's body was already moving. Her arm swept up, aiming the flashlight at her enemy's face, and then her thumb clicked the switch.

Light exploded in the dim basement and the Hare shrieked. The gun roared deafeningly loud in the cramped basement. Paige flinched, sure that she'd feel a bullet tear through her body. Instead, it ricocheted off one of the pipes with a metallic whine.

And *still,* Lily wouldn't move! The Hare turned, shielding her eyes.

Which was all Paige needed. Flipping her silly 'combat flashlight' around, she slammed its baton-like end upward.

Shattering the ceramic plaque into a dozen pieces

Shouts and roars rang out upstairs—then a man's scream of horror. Once more, the Hare raised her gun. Paige stepped in front of Jake, shielding him as best she could... and then, something moved with shocking speed.

Lily closed the distance to the Hare with a flawless somersault. Like some deadly ballerina, she rolled to her feet, fist swinging in a vicious uppercut that leveled the Witch.

Kneeling over her fallen foe, the Wolf shot Paige a toothy grin. "Nice job, Omega. Here." The Shifter kicked her enemy's gun across the floor. Paige took it, shaking with relief and adrenaline. "Protect your kid. And if she wakes up before I'm back, shoot her."

With that, she Shifted and, with a howl of terrible joy, bounded up the stairs to join the battle.

CHAPTER 13

There were sounds. Terrible sounds that would haunt her dreams.

The crash of a car ramming its way through a plate-glass window. Gunshots. Lots of gunshots. A roar so loud it seemed to shake the floor. Snarls, yelps, screams of pain. A man's voice, thin and terrified, begging for mercy. Cut short by another gunshot.

Down in the cellar, Paige hugged her terrified son and waited for the horror to stop. Knowing that she might be forced to add to it if someone came down those stairs.

When the noise ended, total silence enveloped the house, as terrible in its own way as the battle before. Gun clenched tightly in her fist, she shivered, dreading the moment when she'd learn who had won—and whether she'd lost a lover or a new friend.

Footsteps staggered across the floor above her and the door clicked open. Then a familiar, welcome voice said, "Paige? You guys okay?"

"Lily!" A flash of relief—until she realized that something was badly wrong. Neither dark humor nor wild joy colored the Wolf's words. For the first time, she sounded somber. "Is Rex okay? Are you all right?"

"We're alive and they're not, so... yeah. Guess that's 'all right.'" The cot squeaked as Paige rose to her feet and the Wolf quickly added, "Don't come up here. It's a mess. You and your boy don't want to see this."

Something sailed down the stairs and landed with a metallic rattle. "Cuffs. For the Witch. Backup's coming. I'll let you know when it's safe to leave."

Why wasn't Rex telling her that? Where was he? She heard the Wolf retrace her path with slow, pained steps. But no heavy tread joined her. Nothing that could belong to a Bear.

Don't panic. Lily said he's alive. Help's coming.

Fighting back her own fears, she cuffed the Hare's arms around a stair board and retreated back to Jake.

Fifteen minutes later, roars filled the air. Motorcycles. A *lot* of them. Lily's sharp, high howl rang out—and a dozen answered her. The bass howls of the male Wolves and quite a few soprano ones as well.

Lily's Pack had arrived. And, as she said, they all came. Men and women, from Alpha to Omega.

Still, she caught no hint of Rex in the confused welter of shouts, voices, and engines. Boot heels clicked across the floor and when the door opened this time, a strange man's voice called down. "Miss Hall? I'm Aaron King. Lily's father. May I come down?"

"Yes!" Jake pressed himself close against her and she gave him a hug.

A slender man with a salt and pepper ponytail descended, dressed heel to chin in black leather. As he passed the unconscious Hare, he murmured, "You're not fooling anyone, woman. I know you're awake. I'll deal with you in a minute."

Paige gulped. Actually, the Hare *had* fooled someone: her. Silently, she blessed Lily for giving her the handcuffs.

"Is Rex okay?" she asked him, fighting to keep the fear from her voice.

"Yes."

Oh, thank heaven! Paige closed her eyes, weak with relief.

"He's been shot four or five times, but–"

"What?" she squawked. "How can you call that 'okay'?"

Her outrage startled the Wolf and his lips wrinkled back in a brief snarl before he composed himself. "I say it because I know Bears and how hard they are to kill. Your Mate will be fine."

Mate. There was that word again. He assumed she meant something to Rex. That they were more than casual lovers. She ought to correct him, to assure him that the Bear didn't love her. But she couldn't.

Because that title felt too good. Full of love and promise. *Mate.* A fierce, uncivilized word that tied her to Rex's wild life.

Let them think she'd earned it, even if that wasn't true. It made her feel a part of this strange new world.

"We're getting him in the van now. Do you want to ride with him? One of my Pack can take your boy."

The very hint of that sent Jake into a panic. "Mommy, no! Don't leave me!"

"I won't, sweetheart. I promise." After a quick kiss, she asked, "I think it would be better if Jake rode with him too."

The Alpha Wolf shrugged. "Sure. As long as he doesn't mind the sight of blood. A *lot* of it."

Uh, no. That would be a problem. "Why don't I follow you in Rex's Jeep, then?"

"Because it's stuck halfway through the living room wall."

Oh, right. That huge crash… "Could I ask one of your Pack for a ride to the hospital?"

"Sure. Are you two hurt?"

"No. For Rex."

Again, the ghost of a smile made his lips twitch. "We're taking Rex home, not to a hospital."

"After being shot a half-dozen times? You've got to be kidding!"

"Miss Hall." King crouched down before her, gazing up with a gentle amusement. "I understand you're a new Mate. You need to remember that you don't know anything about us. You don't know what punishment a Bear can take or how fast they heal. So, trust us. We're Fairburn's friends. We'll take care of him, the Shifter way. Okay?"

Though it broke her heart, she nodded. Slowly.

And promised herself she'd find a way to make him pay if he was wrong.

PAIGE AND JAKE RODE BACK TO REX'S HOUSE IN A MOTORCYCLE sidecar. A trip that Jake enjoyed a lot more than she did. Aaron King was extremely careful. The driver picked them up behind the house and whisked them away quickly, before her son caught a glimpse of the devastation and blood. When they pulled up to Rex's house, King strolled over. "Miss Hall, could you tell the babysitter she can go?"

Oh, right. Judy was still here, minding the Fairburn children.

"And tell the kids to go to their rooms. I don't think they need to see their father like this."

Not after the losses those poor little souls had already suffered, no.

Holding Jake's anxious hand, she shooed the kids upstairs and left her son to give them a G-rated version of the story. Then, she hustled Judy out.

Her neighbor eyed the seedy-looking band of Wolves.

"Um, hey. Paige? Mr. Fairburn knows they sell weed in dispensaries now, right? You don't need to deal with, uh, *certain people*, anymore."

"They're not drug dealers," she assured her. "They're his friends."

"Uh huh."

Judy didn't sound persuaded. Probably thought Rex was after something a little 'harder' than marijuana.

Whatever. She didn't have time for foolishness now. "We're *fine*."

"Uh huh." Her neighbor edged toward her car, biting her lip.

"You're not going to do anything silly, like call the police, right?"

Her friend shot her a wounded look. "Dude, no! I would never narc on someone. You know that."

"Good. Because everyone's friends here. We're cool."

"Cool. Okay." Lips pinched, eyes clouded with doubt, Judy drove off, gazing sadly into the rear view mirror as she pulled away.

Once the babysitter was gone, the Wolves got to work. The back doors of their panel van flipped open and Lily hobbled out. Right arm in a sling and sporting a bandage that ran from her nose to her ear. Paige's stomach flipped at the sight. But when Lily spotted her, she still managed a bruised smiled.

"Heya, Omega. Hanging in there?"

'Omega', not 'Puppy-Girl'. It seemed she'd been promoted. "I guess so." Paige sidled close, trusting the Wolf Princess to give her an honest answer. "How bad is it?"

"Serious but not critical. Hang onto your undies, though, because if you haven't seen busted up Shifters, it's gonna look way worse than it really is."

Four Wolves clustered around the rear of the panel van. Slowly, they hauled out a stretcher.

Rex lay upon it, stripped naked. Gauze wound about his shoulders, head, chest, stomach and left leg. Every inch of skin not covered in bandages was spattered with blood.

How could anyone survive that? A high ringing tone filled her ears and the world grew hazy. She should never have let them bring him home. He needed a hospital, a doctor. She had to get him away from these nutcases.

As her fear reached a panic pitch, one of his eyes flickered open. A low, menacing growl rumbled from his chest.

Aaron King was at his side in an instant. "You're home, Fairburn. You're safe. It's over."

Rex swatted him away weakly. "Paige? Where is she?"

One word was all it took. Fear vanished, washed away by joy. "Rex, I'm here." She, too, hurried to his side and caught that bloody hand.

Brown eyes, dark with anguish and worry, searched her face. "Jake?"

"He's safe. We're fine. You saved us."

His hand went limp in hers. Paige held it, and kissed his fingertips.

"Bone-Dog will get you settled and cleaned up," King said. Rex didn't seem to hear. His eyes fluttered once then rolled back in his head and his body relaxed into a frightening stillness.

One that seemed *wrong* to Paige. "Did you give him morphine or something?"

"Nope. That's his Bear." King drew her aside, giving the bearers space to move the stretcher. "It's a good sign. Now that he knows his family is safe, he's... well, I guess you can think of it as 'hibernating'."

"In summer?"

"For Shifters, it's not a winter thing. Bears pull into themselves when they're hurt. They sleep—for days, if needed—and all their energy goes into healing. Wish I could do it," the Alpha grumbled. "Getting laid up sucks."

Four Wolves carried Rex gently into the house. Paige hovered nearby as they washed him and settled him in his bed. Then they left, leaving an unsettling quiet behind them.

King paused on his way out. "You got this?"

She nibbled her lip. "I'm not a nurse."

"He doesn't need one. Watch him. Give him water or soup if he wakes. Other than that, leave him be. Can you do that?"

"Yes." And the children would probably feel better once the house wasn't full of strangers.

"Good." He offered her a scrap of paper. "My number. Any worries, any problems, you call."

With that, the Wolves withdrew.

Leaving her with a wounded Bear and five frightened children.

CHAPTER 14

An old Tom Petty song claimed that 'The waiting is the hardest part'. This time around, Paige didn't agree. Memory hurt more than anything else.

Hers woke her in the middle of the night with dreams of Room 415. Dreams where Novak shot her, or Jake. In one, she leaped from the window to escape him and fell, on and on, endlessly. Screaming.

Yet, her torment paled beside the children's. Their suffering, their pain, made her forget her own misery.

Every one of them had lost a parent. Every one of them knew that sometimes, there was no happy ending. People died. Parents were ripped from your life, never to return. The thought that this might be happening, again, filled them all with a panic that dwarfed her fears.

She helped in every way she could. By holding Eden while she sobbed. By promising little Sam that yes, if Rex died, he could come live with her. By holding them, hugging them, loving them with all of her heart.

Jake's memories haunted him too. The first night, he woke in a panic, screaming, sure he was back in the basement, and it took her far too long to run from Rex's room to his side. After that, Paige built a 'fort' out of sheets and chairs in the sickroom. All six of them slept together, in a nest of blankets and sleeping bags. No one would wake alone until this was over.

During the day, chores helped. Paige found little things the kids could do to 'take care' of Rex. Sam, Nate, and Jake picked flowers for him. Eden cooked soup with her and waited, lukewarm broth in hand, for any chance to feed her dad. Together, they made cookies, a sugary morale boost all the children loved. Only Micah, at age ten, proved a problem. He wanted 'real' work, 'adult' tasks. When she learned that the house had a security camera, Paige assigned him to watching it. Silly though it was, the little Bear-to-be reveled in the idea of protecting his family. He sat before the screen for hours every day, scanning the land around them for enemies.

In the evenings, they huddled together, watching tv bundled under blankets. Cartoons lulled the children while Paige sat comforting them with her presence. Always alert for any sound, any sign, that Rex stirred.

All day, Paige was there for them. Only at night, in the darkest hours, could she let herself grieve. She would slip out from the tangled nest of sleeping children and pull a chair up to Rex's bed. There, holding his hand, she could finally let her own tears fall. Silently, with no sobs to disturb the children she needed to protect. Each night, those tears wore down her grief. Softening its sharp edges. Dulling it. Until, at last, she could wipe her face and return to the blanket fort, strong again for the little ones.

For the most part, they were alone. The Donnellys stopped by to check on Rex—and to tell her that Novak was 'taken care of.' Paige didn't ask what that meant. The Hare had cooperated; Finn would share her information once Rex was awake. Only the nameless Rat, the 'fixer', remained at large. That news infuriated Micah and sent him back to his vigil at the security cameras.

Bone-Dog, field medic for the Sand Pack, also visited daily to check on Rex's bandages. Each time, he assured them that all was well. He listened patiently to the children's tales of how they 'helped', and praised the work of their little 'Pack'. Those visits left the kids glowing with pride, and Paige cherished that almost as much as the Wolf's nursing.

For three days, they waited and grieved, each in their own way. The weekend passed, Monday dawned. Then, while Paige carefully trimmed the crusts off a half-dozen sandwiches, a little shriek split the air.

"Mom!" Eden screamed. "Dad's awake!"

What had the girl called her? But even as Paige noticed that telling word, it slipped from her mind. She was running, sprinting, stumbling down the hall, to Rex's room.

When she burst through the doorway, the Bear was sitting up in bed. His daughter sat beside him, arms around his chest, hugging him with all her strength.

"Eden, careful!" she gasped.

Rex pulled the girl close, a big, pain-free smile splitting his broad face. "I'm fine. Good as new."

The boys spilled in now, drawn by their sister's cry. They leaped on the bed, scrambled across the 'wounded' man, hugging him. Shocked by his sudden return to health, Paige could only stare. Jake held back too, shy, until Rex spotted him and waved him over. "How you doing? Are you all right?" he asked, as he ruffled the boy's hair.

Jake allowed that touch, nervous but happy. "Uh huh. We rode back in a motorcycle car."

Rex beamed at her over her son's head, a sight that set her heart hammering. "Bet that was fun."

When she could finally pry the kids off their father, she

took them away for lunch. Rex held back. "I need to shower and get these bandages off." He frowned down at his chest. "Not looking forward to that. Bone-Dog, that dumbass, used too much tape. I'll have to pull half my chest hair off."

Sam dissolved into giggles. "Dad said 'ass'!" he announced. In case anyone had missed it.

Paige shooed them to the kitchen. As they ate, a few startled, irate yelps echoed down the stairs. Each one set the kids snickering. Fifteen minutes later, Rex joined them, rubbing his chest.

"Scalped!" Micah teased.

"Eh, shaddup or I'll scalp *you*," his father grumbled.

She'd made more sandwiches. Good thing, because Rex began to gobble them down at a pace that would make a Wolf proud. Paige couldn't stop staring at him. He was fine. Healthy, happy, whole... looking no worse than he had Friday, in her house.

Rex caught her staring and washed his sandwich down with a gulp of lemonade. "King did tell you Bears heal fast, right? Because I *will* have words with him if he forgot."

"No, he told me. It's just...." She waved helplessly. "It's hard to believe. Until you see it."

With their dad's return, the kids were full of plans. They should go to the mall! They should play video games! Together! Everybody! They should go swimming, at Totten! (The Attack of the Amoeba Monster had ruined Sweetwater for them, and as for the Olympic pool in their back yard...) "I don't even know why I built the damned thing," Rex sighed to her. "Nobody uses it."

Paige loved it all. The sight of the family, together. The way the children swarmed around their father, adoringly. The love that lit his face as they came to him with their crises and complaints.

Yet, even as the balm of the Fairburns' love melted her heart, a gentle pain arose.

"Jake and I should probably head home," she told him. "We're eating all your food."

"No." With a chop of his hand, Rex killed that idea. Dead. "You two need to stay here until it's safe."

"But...."

"No. Out of the question." He killed the idea again with another chop. Deader this time. "You're not going out there where the Fangs could grab you or your boy. It's safer here with me. I'll take care of you, I promise."

"I know you will," she told him, her voice soft. "You proved that."

"Then you'll stay?"

"Sure. As long as you want me to."

Paige gulped in shock at her own words. That sounded... odd. Too open-ended. Like she was fishing for an invitation to move in permanently. Yet Rex simply nodded and said, "Good. I called the Donnellys. They're heading over now to give us a briefing on what happened."

'Us.' Not 'him'. Pride made her heart swell. "Great. I'll, uh, bring my combat flashlight."

Rex chuckled, eyes sparkling. "You didn't ditch that stupid thing? It looked like it weighed a ton."

"Are you kidding? Nobody's taking it away from me. Heck, I plan to be buried with it! That 'thing' saved Lily's life! *And* I broke a spell with it!"

That was news to him. And so, while they waited, she told him her version of Jake's rescue.

By the time she finished, their guests had arrived. Kids were banished to the tv room and the four adults shut themselves in Rex's office.

"Let's start with the bad news," Finn said. "We didn't catch that Rat. We know his name is 'Freeman' but that's about it."

So, Jake's kidnapper is still at large. Paige shivered, glad that Rex had offered her shelter.

"I nailed Novak, the Wolf. He grabbed one tote of artifacts and took off, but I caught him."

Nobody asked what had happened to him. Paige didn't care. The man was vile and sadistic.

Bree leaned forward and caught her eye. "Paige, did you see the artifacts they kept in Room 415?"

"Yes. I was trying to take some pictures when I got caught."

The Hare beamed with delight. "Oh, I was hoping you'd say that. Do you know what was in the top totes?"

"A couple dozen Zuni fetishes. Little stone animal carvings," she added, when the Witch frowned. "And a bunch of Ancestral Puebloan pots."

"These ones?" Bree whipped out a phone and scrolled through a series of pictures.

"Um…no. I didn't see those things."

As Finn whooped with delight, his wife explained. "See, Novak only had time to grab one tote. Either he took the top one, or…."

"…or the most important one!" Paige finished.

"Exactly. And if these weren't in the top tote, they've got to be something special."

"So, what exactly did he grab?" Rex asked.

"Buncha crap," the Dragon replied.

Bree scowled. "They're not crap. They're all magical."

"I stand corrected," Finn grumbled. "Buncha magical things that look like all the other crap."

His wife rolled her eyes. "I admit, we can't tell why these pots are special. But they must be."

"Unless totes got moved after Paige left," Rex added. "Sorry to rain on the parade, but it's possible."

"It is," Bree admitted. "The Sedona Warren offered to do a

more formal examination of the items. If it's okay with you, Finn and I will rent a U-Haul and cart all those relics down to them. Maybe someone can find a clue."

The offer seemed to puzzle Rex. "Why are you asking me? They're not my artifacts."

"Because if I don't get *somebody's* permission," Finn said with a hard grin, "every Shifter gossip will sputter about how the awful First Flight swooped in and stole *our* relics. You called the Shifter meeting. This stuff was found in your resort. In my book, that means *you* make the call."

"Take 'em, then," Rex said. "And if anyone bitches, send them to me. By the way, do we have *any* idea what the Fangs are up to? What do defaced kivas and a blob monster have to do with stolen pots?"

It was a question that worried Paige too.

The Donnellys hesitated, and it was Bree who spoke first. "We do. Paige, the Hare you captured spilled her guts in exchange for a more merciful sentence. As we suspected, the Fangs are snatching up as many relics as they can find. They brought them to that safe house, where she ID'd the magical ones. Freeman took those to Novak, who, she believes, shipped them on to the Worm in charge of this operation."

"And the blob?" Paige asked. "The vandalism?"

"Practice." Bree's face grew pinched and worried.

"For what?"

"*Sipapus aren't* Wellsprings. They're not meant to summon things into this world. In fact, on their own, they help spirits from this world pass on to the Other Side. The Fangs are trying to change that. To figure out a way to pry them open and twist them in ways their makers never intended."

Rex winced. "So, they're trying to turn *sipapus* into Wellsprings?"

"No." The Hare chose her next words carefully. "They're

trying to turn them into temporary gates through which they can summon…things."

"I get it," Rex said. "Like that blob."

"Something much worse." Even the big Dragon lowered his voice. "That blob was only a test run. The Fangs' true goal is to summon one creature. One big, ugly thing."

"What is it?" Paige whispered.

With a grimace, the Dragon shrugged. "That Hare didn't know. But whatever it is, it's bad."

And the Fangs of Apophis wanted to summon it.

In their back yard.

CHAPTER 15

After dinner, they all toasted marshmallows over the fire pit. The kids made sure Rex knew every single thing that had happened while he was out. How Eden made soup for him *all by herself*, with totally no help *at all* from Paige. How Jake came up with the idea for the blanket fort and what Sam did to make it 'betterer'. All of the little ones swore that they were going to stay up all night. Yet, time and food proved them wrong. One by one, they dozed off and were carried to bed.

Which left just Paige and Rex, alone by the fire.

It should have been pure romance, a perfect, intimate moment. Instead, she found herself floundering in awkward silence.

Oh, she *felt* passion's siren call. Moon and fire cast long shadows across Rex's face. He lounged on his chair with the casual ease of a man in his den, confident and in control. How she longed to join him. To slip her hands around that broad, powerful chest. To snuggle close and feel his arms weave around her, protecting her from all the world.

Yet there they sat, him on one side of the fire, her on the

other. Proper. Polite. Cool. A world apart.

Rex was the first to break that uncomfortable ice. "Can I get you something to drink?"

"No, thank you. I'm not a big fan of whiskey."

"Got some nice wine too."

"Sorry," she said with an apologetic smile. "I've tried that too and wasn't fond of it."

"You 'tried' wine?" For some reason, that seemed to amuse him. "What kind?"

"Both of them. Red *and* white. Didn't like either. Too bitter."

Rex's lips twitched. "Hang on. I've got one that isn't 'bitter'...." When he returned, he held two enormous glasses. "Humor me, okay? Try one sip."

One couldn't hurt, right? Especially, a small one.

Paige knew, vaguely, that there were things you did before you drank wine. Sniff a cork, wave the glass around, that sort of stuff. The cork was nowhere to be found, so she gave the goblet a little waggle and then poured the tiniest bit into her mouth and gulped.

The taste that filled her mouth startled her. Light yet earthy, touched with a hint of raspberry. Rex was right! Not bitter at all! Paige took a second, larger, sip and held it in her mouth, letting that smooth, velvety flavor surround her tongue.

He leaned back to enjoy her confusion. "Good?"

"Actually...yes!"

"That's what I thought. You don't hate wine. You hate *bad* wine. This is a pinot noir, and it's very, very good."

At first, they sat in a comfortable wordless peace. Sipping wine, watching the moon, and listening to the crackle of the blaze. Yet, slowly, gently, the wine worked its magic. Paige started talking. First, about simple things. His beautiful home. How much she adored his children. The wine's glow spread through her, loosening knots deep within her soul. Freed, she spoke of other, deeper matters. Leonard. Her hopes for Cortez. The fear—and yes, joy—she'd felt since learning about Shifters.

For the most part, Rex just listened. Now and then, he tossed out a question. She asked a few of her own. About his wife and his parents. Each time, he deftly changed the subject. If she wished to bare her soul, he was eager to learn. His own past, however, remained a secret.

When the bottle stood empty and she drained the last drops from her glass, he smiled at her. "Probably time for us to go to bed."

Paige beamed at him. Why, yes! Yes, it was! Rex was so damned clever!

"A real bed this time?" she asked. "Or the pool again?"

"The pool? What do you… Oh." His mouth opened into a perfect 'O' of surprise. "Shit, I'm sorry. I actually meant 'bed.' As in, sleep."

"You want to go to sleep? Now?" Her disapproving stare was only slightly unsteady.

"Yes, I do."

"Well, I don't!" she chirped, the words slipping out before she could catch them.

"Paige." Laughter and exasperation warred in his voice. "I'm not taking advantage of you when you've had too much wine."

"I haven't had too much wine!" she protested. "I've had…*enough!*"

"Enough for what, exactly?"

"Enough to stop running." Under her somber gaze, his amusement died away, fading to something far more serious. "Enough to dare tell you, Rex Fairburn, that I want you. I don't care if you're out of my league…."

"Who said that?" Indignation lit his face. "Tell me you

don't believe that!"

She didn't bother to answer. "I don't care if I'm just a housekeeper and you're a millionaire. I want you. Now. Tonight."

"Paige," he sighed, shaking his head. "I can't. You need to go to bed."

Tossing her nose in the air, she threw her arms wide. "Well, if you think I'm so darned drunk, I guess you'll have to carry me to bed, won't you?"

Finally, her teasing won a sly grin from him. "Is that supposed to be a challenge?"

With no more warning, he crouched beside her. Strong arms wrapped around her and suddenly, she was flying, tossed into the air. Paige shrieked with delight as he caught her tight against his chest. Rex tried for a frown—but he couldn't quite pull it off. "And now, to bed!" he growled.

Which gave her a couple of minutes to work on *her* plan....

She wove her own arms around his neck, cuddling close. With her cheek against his throat, she could feel the beat of his heart. A rhythm that grew quicker, hungrier at the feel of her breasts pressed against his chest.

As he kicked open the door to the living room, she kissed him on his jaw. Letting the warmth of her breath whisper against his ear.

"Paige...," he groaned.

Lower her lips moved. Down, tasting the taut muscles of his neck. Nuzzling beneath his collar to savor the hidden planes of his shoulder. A pause and then her mouth rose to his throat again. Teasing, delighting in the hard pulse that her touch roused. As he reached the stairs, her mouth rose too. Her lips closed around the lobe of his ear, sucking, and his breath grew ragged. Playfully, she nipped him and was rewarded with a low moan of desire.

At the top of the stairs, he paused. Her seduction was a delicious honey that slowed him, trapped him. A snare his body welcomed.

"Paige... I shouldn't...." His words, heavy with the longing that sang in his blood, struggled vainly against his desire.

"Why not?" she whispered with a kiss. "Why shouldn't we take what we both want?"

"But what will–"

"Hush." A finger across his lips silenced him. "Forget the future. We're here, now."

And neither of them doubted what they wanted at that moment. The last of his reservations crumbled as he held her.

"You're right. Tomorrow can take care of itself."

Passion spurred him fast, bold, down the hall. The door to his room lay open, moonlight flooding through its floor-to-ceiling windows. There, before the desert and the night sky, he carried her to the bed and laid her down upon its soft linens.

Drained of color by the moon's cool light, he stood above her, painted in black and white like a hero from some old movie. Slowly, he pulled his shirt off. Chiseled abs appeared and thick, curly chest hair. Each movement made those muscles flex and gave her another, fuller glimpse of his tantalizing body.

When he tossed the shirt aside, she repaid him. One by one, she popped open the buttons of her blouse. Teasing him, inch by inch, with glimpses of her bra and breasts. As the last button surrendered beneath her fingers, she arched her back. The shirt slid across her skin as he stared, intoxicated by the first hints of her nakedness. Up her breasts rose, and she tugged the shirt off. With a flick of her wrist, she sent it flying to join his forgotten clothes.

And then, it was his turn. Back and forth they went, each

peeling off one piece of clothing. His pants, revealing the hard, firm curves of his butt. Her bra, releasing her eager breasts to the moon's kiss. Every pass stripped away another piece of cloth, another barrier that kept them apart.

The last veil was thrown aside, leaving nothing to hide them. Her laying on the bed, eager, the swell of her hips and breasts echoed by the pillows that propped her up. Him standing tall, hard and sculpted, his cock beginning to jut with arousal.

He settled beside her, propping himself up on one elbow. One hand stroked her flank and stomach. In its wake, her skin tingled with anticipation. Under its caresses, she felt herself grow damp. Soon, their union would be complete.

And yet….

And yet, Paige found herself wanting more. Yearning, longing for this moment to last, for her need to grow hotter, fiercer. Years with Leonard had taught her the rhythm of sex. How it ended too soon, before she'd known the heights of true pleasure.

Kiss me, she almost begged him. *Keep this passion alive for just a few minutes longer!*

But no. With firm hands, he slid her legs apart. Her plea died unspoken as he lowered himself and kissed her breasts. Soft, warm lips circled her nipple, sucking. Delicious, wonderful…if only she didn't know that this signaled the end of their love-making.

Lower he slid, kissing hips and flanks. And then, Rex Fairburn did something that Leonard had never dared in all their years together. Crouched between her thighs, he bent down over her womanhood and kissed it.

A bolt of purest pleasure—hot, fierce—coursed through her body. She could feel the heat of his breath against the short fuzz that covered her most private parts. Hinting at exquisite pleasures yet to come.

Higher he kissed her, along the bottom of her belly. Lips teasing, so close. Then his hand stole between her legs. Another rush of excitement swept over her as his fingers explored her damp hair. Stroking, rubbing.

A low moan escaped her as those fingers pulled away. And immediately, his mouth answered her wordless plea.

His face pressed against her pussy, kissing, suckling closer. Beneath its touch, the folds that hid her clitoris slipped apart, admitting him. His tongue flickered out, lapping at that hidden treasure.

Shudders swept through her with each sweet, wet stroke. Paige wailed, her fingers knotted in the tangled bed sheets, writhing against him as her helpless body tossed. And when his lips closed tight around her nub, sucking….

"Stop!" she gasped. "Stop! I can't…."

Sweet agony as the pleasuring ceased. She struggled to keep herself from being swept over the edge, from being swallowed by her own desire before he had been fulfilled.

But her cries, the delirious, animal movements of her body, had roused him fully. Rex raised himself above her. Hard, eager, hot. And then he plunged into her welcoming cleft.

Teased to the edge of rapture, she cried out as he filled her. Driven by their shared need, she wrapped her legs tightly against him. Riding each stroke. Holding him within her for one moment, until his powerful legs broke free. Only to drive in, again and again, until, with a pure, wail of joy, she came.

Another thrust… a second, as she floated, caught in the waves of pleasure. Then, with a moan of wild delight, he came, joining her in release.

Panting, he collapsed beside her. Paige curled against his chest and together, they cuddled, beneath the moon's approving gaze.

CHAPTER 16

The morning sun rose over a scene that the Fairburn family had not seen in years. For once, there was no sign of the traditional insanity of breakfast.

Rex surveyed the dining room, numb with shock. Toast, pancakes, eggs and juice all appeared at the same time. All hot—and all unique. Big flapjacks for him and Micah. A plate of small animal-shaped pancakes for the little kids. And the eggs! Sunnyside up for him, over-easy for the kids. Plus, 'baked into shoe leather' for little Sam. There was even a plate of no-crust toast, which Nate happily dunked into his egg yolks, to his brother's disgust.

Paige, the author of this miracle, finally joined them. "How did you manage this?" he murmured. "I'm lucky if *one* thing is warm by the time I get it to the table."

"Magic," she said, then burst out laughing at the look on his face. "I'm joking, silly! It's just practice."

"I'm not so sure about that. Personally, my money's on magic!"

Another bite of pancakes, thick with maple syrup. A chunk of crisp, buttery toast. A gulp of sharp, rich coffee to wash it down. Rex fell silent, lost in the simple pleasures of a perfectly prepared breakfast.

This was heaven. Let other men drown themselves in the luxuries of New York and Los Angeles. For him, this was as good as life got. Food, warm and tasty. His children surrounding him, happy and chattering. And his... his....

MATE!

...woman beside him. The last echoes of the night's passion lingered in his body.

It was perfect. For the first time since Ashley's death, he felt truly happy. Not 'content'. Not 'strong enough to face tomorrow alone'. Not 'good enough not to bum the kids out'.

Happy.

Today, he dared to hope that tomorrow might be more than 'endurable'—it might be wonderful and special. A dream lost to him these four long years.

All because of her. Paige Hall. Over his steaming mug, Rex studied her. The soft lines of her round, sweet face. That one wayward bang that kept flopping down in front of her eyes. The graceful curves of her long neck and the supple strength of her tanned body.

Our Mate, his Bear rumbled, filled with simple delight.

For once, he didn't have the heart to disagree. He *could* make a life with this woman. Together, they could weave another thread into this large, blended family. With her by his side, the future would be a promise—not an enemy that needed to be defeated or survived.

If that was what she wanted.

He knew she wanted *him*. Last night left no doubts on that score. She loved the children already, with the open heart of a simple, pure soul. She even loved *him*, despite his temper and awkwardness. He believed what she told him during Jake's rescue (even if he hadn't had the time—or the courage—to admit that he, too, felt something deeper than friendship).

In fairy tales, that would be enough. True love always led to happily ever after, right?

Unfortunately, they lived in the real world. Here, love didn't always sweep you away to a shining white castle. Sometimes, it dragged you to the twisted, burning wreck of a car on Route 491.

That memory cast a bitter chill across the morning's peace.

Stop it. Ashley would kick your ass if she heard this whining. She'd tell you to move on. To keep living. To find a Mate, a mother for her children. Someone to love them and care for them when she couldn't.

Someone to care for *him* too.

A hand stroked his arm, drawing him out of that brooding. "Hey. You okay?" Paige asked.

"Yeah. Just thinking. About, uh, this mess." Better a lie than to admit he'd been meditating on his dead wife. He was about to apologize for letting the food she'd cooked grow cold. When he glanced at his plate, though, he realized that he'd wolfed it all down.

Good thing I'm a man who can brood and eat at the same time.

Rising, he gave Paige's hand a squeeze. "You guys finish up. I'll be in my office. I want to look over those pictures one last time."

As he left, the sounds of home swelled behind him.

What he wouldn't give to hear that again. Tomorrow, and the next day, and every day, until the kids were grown.

Then grand-cubs, his Bear suggested. *And great-grand-cubs.*

"Rein it in there, buddy," he chuckled. "You're getting ahead of yourself."

Before any of that could happen, he and Paige needed to talk. By itself, love wasn't enough. They'd known each other for less than two weeks and already, Paige had been attacked by some demonic monstrosity, fended off a grizzly with a stick, and had her son kidnapped. Who wanted that kind of shit in their life? Who would be willing to risk her life—and the life of her precious son?

She loved him, sure. But did she love him *that* much?

Or would the lure of a quiet, peaceful, *safe* life prove too strong? He couldn't blame her if it did.

Settling down in front of his computer, he paged through pictures of the relics from Novak's tote. No matter how closely he studied them, he found himself agreeing with Finn Donnelly. It was crap. A whole bunch of valuable, magical, important... crap. Each nameless object looked exactly like every other piece of priceless ancient junk.

Some time later, a soft rap interrupted his pointless musing. Paige poked her head in, smiling. "Hey. Mind company? I'd love to see those artifacts."

"Well, that makes one of us!" He scooted his chair to the side and waved her over. "Sure. Come take a look."

Once more, he started the slideshow. This time, though, to an appreciative audience. Paige oohed and aahed at each one like the stupid pots were the Crown Jewels of England. "Look at that! There isn't a single crack on it!" And, "Oh, isn't that design lovely? Look at the sharp contrast between the white and black!"

One bowl (the most boring one, in his estimation) fascinated her. "That is so odd!"

"Not really. I think we got forty bowls, all told. Hell, there were three in Novak's tote."

"It's not the bowl, it's the picture."

The bottom of the bowl was 'decorated' (if you could use

that term) with a bunch of rectangles. "Guess I'm not a big fan of the famous Puebloan painting 'Boxes in a Bowl.'"

"They're buildings, silly," she giggled. "Which is strange because most Ancestral Puebloan art was abstract."

"So, this bowl is unusual because we can actually tell what they were trying to draw?" He struggled to keep a smile off his face.

"Well, yes. And because of this." She pointed at the largest rectangle.

"I gotta admit, that is a large box."

"Building. One with six floors."

Earnest and intent, Paige stared at him like that ought to mean something. So somber, so serious that he wanted to pull her close and kiss her until she laughed. "You have no idea why that's important, do you?"

"Nope," he admitted.

"Cliff dwelling houses are often four to five stories tall—but never six. This," she pointed at the picture, "is someplace special and unique."

That killed his teasing mood at once. "So, it's one place. Someplace we could find."

Paige nodded. "I have this weird sense of *déjà vu*. I swear I've been there!"

While she mulled that over, he opened a browser and did a few quick scans for 'six-story Puebloan ruins'. Nothing. Paige was right: the building in the bowl was either imaginary—or unique and unknown.

"Sorry, babe, I can't find–"

"Ooh!" Delight lit her eyes, rousing a fire inside of him. One that didn't give a damn about some stupid pot. "I remember."

With no apology, she snatched the keyboard out of his hands. Bemused, Rex watched as she navigated to some bulletin board called 'Pot Hounds.' (A name that conjured images of a very different kind of 'pot' in his mind…). A few searches and a lot of scrolling later, Paige crowed with delight.

"Here! On the 'Oddest Find' thread, PotBoi52 posted that he found a six-story building in a small, partially collapsed ruin. No one believed him, because the top three stories were ruined, and he didn't have any pictures."

"Pics or it didn't happen," Rex agreed.

"But…." Scroll, scroll, scroll. "There! He gave directions to the site. Nobody followed up on it because it was a twenty-eight-mile hike, one way."

"How did this lunatic find it?"

"No idea." Paige's eyes were bright with glee. "But it's got to be our bowl building."

Twenty-eight miles. *One* way. Damn, that was a trip! "Okay, I guess I can buy a dirt bike and check it out."

"By yourself? Shouldn't you call Finn Donnelly?"

"No." Like *he* needed a babysitter! "I can check out one stupid building."

Paige folded her arms across her chest, scowling. "Uh huh. How good is your orienteering?"

"My Oreo-what?"

"That's what I thought. Get two bikes. We'll go together."

"Out of the question!" He and his Bear both growled. "It might be dangerous."

"If it's dangerous, you ought to take Finn," she said, her voice honey-sweet. Rex scowled; he knew a trap when he saw it. "If it's safe enough for you to go alone, then you'll need me to follow PotBoi52's directions."

There was a certain logic to that…one he didn't like. "Here's the problem: we don't know if it's safe or not."

"Any sign of trouble and I leave, immediately."

"What about the kids?" Surely, that would deter her?

"There's Judy…." Paige's nose wrinkled. "Though, after

she let Jake get kidnapped, I'd rather skip her. Aren't there any Shifters you trust?"

"Well…." Dammit. He hated to admit it, but she had a point. If he didn't find this place, he'd wander the desert for days. "I could ask SueSue Mint to look after them."

"Is she another Bear?"

"No, a Rat."

"You want a Rat to watch our kids?" His Mate radiated doubt—and that was *before* she'd had a chance to see the Rat's shifty face.

But Rex knew SueSue and how much of a bum steer her Kind got. "Rats are survivors. If anything happens, she'll get our kids out. We might not ever see them again," he added, his eyes sparkling, "because she spirited them away to a nuke-proof bunker somewhere in the depths of the Mojave Desert. But dammit, they *will* be safe!"

Paige's carefree laugh brought a smile to his face. "Sold. Rat babysitter it is."

"Then let's go see if there's anything important at this ruin!"

CHAPTER 17

Perched on her shiny new Honda dirt bike, Paige imagined herself driving past Lily King.

The Wolf would *not* be impressed.

Oh, the bike was pretty enough. Red and silver chrome, gleaming under the hot sun. Paige had a neat new mesh suit, which looked much like a cleaner version of the Wolf's own gear.

That wasn't the problem. The problem was her speed.

Foolishly, she'd assured Rex that she knew how to ride a bike. Which was true. Completely.

Except dirt bikes weren't anything like regular bikes. They were small motorcycles, and as soon as you got them off the pavement, their front wheels wiggled terribly. Rex swore this was normal and she'd get used to it.

In time. Which they didn't have.

And so they crawled across the desolate landscape. Rex could have covered twenty-eight miles in an hour, easy. With her, he puttered slowly toward the ruins. PotBoi52's lousy directions didn't make this any easier. Repeated breaks for orienteering drained even more time away.

Still, it was faster than hiking. No question about that. And Rex was a gentle, patient teacher.

"You sure I can't hop on behind you?" she begged him.

"Nope. Not safe—and it's too much weight."

"But it would be faster."

"You're doing fine," he assured her.

Which was kind. If not accurate.

Once more, she took a compass reading and checked her topo map. Hill to the northwest… check. Ridge running east north-east… check. Which meant….

"There." The ridgeline pointed like an arrow at a small rise of land. "These ruins should be just over that."

If so, the land around them offered no signs. Once more, Paige found herself wondering how on earth PotBoi52 had found this place.

A short drive brought them to the rise. As promised, the far side dropped sharply, forming a barren ravine. Rex surveyed it, frowning. "I don't see any ruins."

"Look there!" Paige's heart soared as she spotted a faint, sloping path winding down the canyon wall.

"We're not seriously walking down that, are we?" her lover growled.

This was a risk she understood… and didn't mind. "Sure. Just watch your footing and follow me." Grumbling wordlessly, he trailed after her. "Remember, people used these trails every day for centuries."

"Uh huh. And how many of them ended up in a heap at the bottom of the gulch?"

Despite his worries, the trail was solid. The Ancestral Puebloans made their 'roads' to last through the ages. Narrow and steep, it wove down and around a bend. As they rounded the curve, Paige's sharp eye picked up the clues she expected. Erosion—there was water here once. Plants thriving in the shadow of the overhang. And finally….

"There!" she crowed with delight.

Rex frowned, dubious. "That's it?"

PotBoi52's unnamed ruin wasn't much to look at. Built under a lip of stone, the tiny site only included four small buildings plus the great tower that had drawn them.

What is this place? It's so small, and so far away from other Puebloan ruins. It must have been very special, once upon a time.

Now, though, it was just sad. Part of the cliff had collapsed centuries ago. The landslide took out the top two stories of the great tower, leaving nothing but a dilapidated stub. Boulders and debris lay scattered everywhere. Once this might have been pretty but now it was just a ratty little pile of rocks.

Still, they were looking for magic, not art. "Let's take a look at the big building," she said.

A hand, big and strong, caught her shoulder. "Me first," the Bear insisted. Something Paige didn't disagree with.

She followed him into the first floor, where a number of footprints stood out clearly in the dust and sand. Scrape marks, too, beneath the hole which led to the second story. Paige knew exactly what those meant. "Somebody brought a ladder down here."

"Which is gone now, so they're not here."

Rex wove his fingers into a 'saddle' for her foot. Then he tossed her up through the opening in the ceiling. Easily, as if she weighed no more than a cat. When she stepped back, he jumped and, with a strength that took her breath away, hauled himself up beside her.

Bare walls and floors surrounded them. No paintings, no pots. Nothing. "I think we wasted a day," Rex sighed.

Paige feared he could be right. "Might as well check the last floor though, since we came so far."

"Sure." Once more, he gave her a boost up. But when she

popped into the third floor, what she saw took her breath away.

Three of the room's walls were blank. But the fourth….

Stylized figures covered the last wall, stick figures like the ancient rock carvings that dotted the south-west. Nothing that belonged in an Ancestral Puebloan site! Yet the picture wasn't carved. It was painted—as if the people who'd lived here copied something even older.

And the image itself…just looking at it sent shivers down her spine.

Scenes from a world-ending apocalypse lined its edges. Villages and crops burned. The bodies of the dead piled high, while the living fled screaming into the desert.

At the heart of the chaos, five figures stood in a circle. Three were clear: a Bear, a Wolf, and a Dragon.

All of those are Shifter Kinds!

The fourth was lost, scraped off in some ancient accident. Only its outstretched arm remained. And the fifth….

A hideous creature writhed in torment, its face twisted into a wordless howl. From its back, a spray of bones fanned out.

Skeletal wings? What's left of wings when they rot away?

All five Shifters reached up toward a symbol she didn't recognize. Arrows radiated up from it, toward the painting's true horror.

One being dominated the upper half of the picture, a great skeletal form that rose out of billowing black clouds. Its maw, full of fangs, gaped wide. Within it, screaming humans slid down its throat, clutching desperately at teeth, at each other. At anything that would keep them from toppling down into the monster's belly. Its hands, tipped with scythe-like claws, swept through the fleeing crowds, snatching up more victims.

"Oh, wow," Paige breathed. "Rex, I found it."

"Found what?" His anxious face appeared below her. "Are you okay?"

"I'm fine. I'm just blown away. There's a huge painting up here and I bet it's what the Fangs were looking for. It seems to show five Shifters summoning a skeletal monster that...."

A chill swept over her, and a sharp pain, as if an icicle had been driven through her heart.

Nemagorix, whispered a voice in her mind. *Not 'skeletal monster.'*

Paige screamed.

With a roar, Rex threw himself at the hole above him. This time, his fingers missed the edge by two inches. "Paige! Jump! I'll catch you."

"I...."

I will not harm you, the voice promised.

Like she was going to believe *that* thing!

But she wasn't going to abandon her mission, either. Quickly, she snatched out her phone and started snapping pictures.

"Paige!" Furious, half mad with his Bear's protective urge, Rex howled up at her. "Screw that! Jump!"

"Hang on!" Two more pictures... three. A cold, alien amusement seemed to radiate off the monstrous figure. "It's just talking. I'm okay."

"Something's talking to you? Oh hell no, that's not 'okay'! Get down here, now!"

Just a couple more. Just a couple.

The monster approved. *You have courage and you are beautiful. It would be a pleasure to wear you.*

'Wear'. The same thing that blob said. Bile burned its way up her throat as she took her last shots.

Somehow, Nemagorix sensed her unease. *Do not fear Union. Great power will be yours. Your desires, your hatreds, will become mine. You will become a goddess. Together, we will take this world and make it pleasing—to us.*

Last shot… done! Paige tucked the phone back, safe, in a pocket and turned her back on the painting.

Destroy the Aegis. Do this thing for me, and I will lay the world at your feet.

"I'll, uh, think about that." She crouched at the edge of the hole and prepared to lower herself down to her anxious lover.

That was when the visions hit her like a tidal wave.

She stood, sipping wine, as the world's finest fashion designers groveled before her, begging her to wear their clothes. Presidents and movie stars stood round, admiring the sleek beauty of her body. Dreaming that, if they were lucky, one of them would be permitted to pleasure her tonight.

Why only one? Nemagorix whispered. *You are their goddess. Take as many as you want.*

Wealth, power…it was hers. With a word, she could kill anyone. No one questioned her, no one challenged her. She had only to gaze upon a rebel and immediately, her power—the thing that 'rode' inside her—shattered their will. They fell to their knees, worshipping her.

Worshipping us. I, and my raiment.

Her knees buckled. Dimly, she felt herself falling, tumbling through the air.

Then a strong pair of arms caught her and pulled her tight against a hard, muscled chest.

"Paige? Are you okay?"

Rex. Rex held her. She buried her face against his chest as those delicious, *horrible* visions faded. The thump of his heart was a drumbeat, and she clung to that sound, to him.

"I am now. Just hold me."

He whisked her outside, far away from that awful painting. Then he knelt, cradling her, and held her until the last of her shivers faded.

When the world steadied itself, she peered up into his worried, craggy face. "The Fangs are trying to summon a creature called 'Nemagorix'. It's not here, but it can speak through that painting. It wants me to find something called 'the Aegis' and destroy it."

"Why?"

"No idea. Nemagorix seemed to think this was obvious and I didn't ask for an explanation."

"Good," Rex muttered. "You stayed way too long as it was. Any idea what this thing wants?"

"To possess me. To 'wear' me."

He snorted with disbelief. "Boy, now isn't *that* a tempting offer."

"Actually, it was." In her mind, she could still feel the whisper of silk across her skin and the heat that had blazed within her, knowing that she could take any man she wanted. "This thing shares its host's desires, pleasures, and emotions. In return, it gives you power. It makes you a god."

Both of them fell silent, imagining what the Fangs could do with such horrific power.

Rex was the first to speak and he proposed a Bear's simple, straightforward plan. "Let's get out of here. Maybe some Hare can get more information out of your pictures."

"Yeah. I never want to see this place again."

Nothing stopped their retreat. No attacks, no spells, no invisible leash to pin them to this tower. Quickly, they hiked back up to the dirt bikes.

While she grabbed her helmet, he checked his phone. "No bars," he sighed. "We'll have to…."

Rex's eyes widened in sudden shock. A red flower bloomed on his chest.

Blood. That's blood.

Time seemed to slow for Paige. In the desert's silence, her lover crumbled to the ground. Only when he lay at her feet did she hear a distant crack.

Rifle.

Sniper rifle.

Their Rat was back.

CHAPTER 18

*P*aige threw herself flat, sprawling face-down in the hot stones. Beneath the pitiless sun, she felt naked. Nothing protected her. No rocks, no trees. The cliff trail was too far away; she'd be cut down before she made it.

The bikes! Dreading a bullet's lethal kiss, she low-crawled behind one of the dirt bikes. From behind its paltry cover, she scanned the desert for any sign of their enemy.

Nothing.

Rats hide. That's what they do.

And this Rat could kill people from a quarter-mile away.

Rex lay fifteen feet from her. Exposed. In the open. The soft rise and fall of his chest was the only sign that he still lived. But there was so much blood! Painted across the rocks… spilling out from beneath his limp form. No one could survive losing that much blood—could they? She had to get to him, bandage him….

And that meant exposing herself to the Rat's attack.

If she didn't, though, Rex would die.

Once, that conundrum would have frozen her in place.

Risk her life for Leonard? Never. Not in a million years. For Rex? Even a week ago, she would have hesitated.

Not anymore. She loved him. Whether he returned her passion or not didn't matter. She couldn't imagine a life without him. Better to be cut down by some despicable Rat and fade away beside him.

Even on this short trip, Rex had insisted they bring an emergency kit. Paige yanked it off the back of the bike. Yet, as she rose, preparing to sprint, a name echoed in her mind.

Jake.

What about Jake? If I die here with Rex, who will care for him? Don't I have to stay alive—for him?

With a moan, she sank down, pressing her forehead against the bike's hot metal. Her love lay dying in the sands before her. But her innocent son waited in town, needing his mother's love and protection.

Rex, she knew, would tell her to leave. To protect the children, all of them, rather than him.

Her heart whispered he was wrong. Love couldn't choose. Love would never sacrifice one part of her family to save another.

She was going to protect *all* of them.

Or die trying.

Three deep breaths to flood her body with oxygen. Then she bolted to her feet and dashed across the desert.

No bullet cut her down before she slammed to her knees beside him. Another scan—no sign of the damned Rat. Where *was* he? Why not shoot her? Was she, a mere human, so useless that he didn't care whether she lived or died?

Once, that thought would have filled her with shame. Now, it summoned a fierce, vengeful fury.

Good. I hope he did *write me off! I'll show him how wrong he is.*

Straining, she rolled the Bear onto his back. Peeling off

his riding jacket, she found a shoulder holster and a BIG gun. That, she set aside. Maybe she could give Mr. Rat Freeman a nasty surprise!

Then she got to work. Wadding thick gauze against the hole in Rex's shoulder. Taping it in place. Struggling to remember her old high school first-aid class.

Every rustle, every weed waving in the wind, made her jump. Paige forced herself not to think about the Rat and his deadly rifle. She did keep glancing up, fearful that he had crept close. If he jumped her before she could shoot him, she had no hope of saving Rex.

Yet the desert remained empty. No sight or sound from the Rat—until she finished bandaging Rex and leaned back on her heels, surveying her work.

Then a thin, grating voice called out from behind a boulder a hundred yards away. "There should be an emergency tarp in that kit. You wanna cover him up; otherwise, he's gonna bake in the sun."

Freeman! Heart hammering, Paige snatched up the gun, took aim, and squeezed the trigger.

Nothing happened. The trigger didn't move an inch.

Safety! Shit! How did you turn one off?

Meanwhile, the Rat continued his monologue. "Since you're waving that thing at me, I'm guessing you don't know how far a .45 slug travels. Let me give you a hint: I'm not in range."

To prove his point, Freeman stepped out from behind the rocks. He wore a grey mottled jacket and hat. Desert camo, she realized. In his arms, he cradled a slender, vicious-looking rifle. The Rat gave it a pat. "Now this beauty has a *much* longer range. And you, ma'am, are well within it. So, I suggest you put your gun down and we have a chat."

There was a little button above the pistol grip. Could that

be the safety? Paige pushed it and couldn't tell if anything happened.

Freeman waited, patient and amused. "Now, if you don't trust my knowledge of guns, you're welcome to test it yourself. Take a shot. I warn you, though, that if you do, I'm gonna shoot that gun out of your hand. You'll probably lose a couple of fingers. Because I'm vengeful like that," he added, with a toothy grin.

Was this a bluff? Could she even hit a target at this distance? Paige licked her lips. Lily hadn't given her a gun when they saved Jake. Maybe shooting people wasn't as simple as the movies made it look.

No, better to try to lure him closer. Slowly, she lowered her weapon. "So, talk. What do you want?"

"I want you to drop that gun, put a tarp over your man so he doesn't die, and then come with me."

"If you didn't want Rex to die, maybe you shouldn't have shot him!" she spat.

"It's all part of the plan, lady."

"What plan? You can't seriously think I'll trust you. Give me a reason to do what you say."

He considered her demand. "Fair enough," he shrugged. "Here's what I'll do. I'll explain all the ways I see this situation ending. You pick the ending you like, and we'll go from there."

"First, you can decide not to cooperate with me. In that case, I'll wander off. Put a couple bullets through you, or your bikes, if I can't shoot you for some reason. You're not carrying a guy his size anywhere."

She hadn't thought of that. Even turning Rex had been hard. "Well, that option sucks," she said, licking her lips.

"I agree. You die. I don't get what I want."

"What *do* you want?" That was the heart of the problem.

"Hostages." The word sent a chill down her spine. "I want

your Bear to live through this and I want to be able to motivate him by threatening his loved ones."

Hadn't Rex talked about that? About how the Fangs of Apophis kidnapped children and Mates to control Shifters? And hadn't he said that the Rats suffered the most?

Paige's eyes lit with hope. "Is that what the Fangs have done to you? Kidnapped your family? I can help! I know a Dragon and I'm sure he could save your people!"

"That's a kind offer, ma'am." From this distance, she couldn't read his face, but a dark, mocking humor colored his words. "Unfortunately for you, not all Rats are blackmailed. Some of us just like this shit."

Okay, fine. At least she wouldn't feel guilty shooting him! "Whatever. So, what's Plan B?"

"Option two is you pretend to agree with me. Then, on the way back to my Jeep, you try some foolishness."

That actually *was* her current plan. Paige waited, wary.

"Maybe you pull it off. Probably not, seeing as how I'm a professional and you're an amateur. But know this: try anything once we leave and I'll kill you."

As if she was afraid of dying! Playing along was her only true hope.

He must have seen the defiance in her eyes, because he continued. "Let me explain why you don't want to try Plan B. Because after I kill you, I'll go get your kids. I'd rather take all of you as hostages, but just the kids works too."

Her stomach roiled at the thought of Jake and the Fairburn children captured by the Fangs. "And what if I cooperate fully?"

"Same situation as Plan B, only you go with the kids. Which means they have someone to care for them and protect them. Hell, you can even try to hatch an escape once you're in the camps. I don't care. After I deliver you, you're someone else's problem."

None of those 'Plans' sounded good to her. But 'Not dying' was the best start. She'd have to keep her wits about her and watch for a way to turn the tables.

"Sold. I pick Plan C." Only the slightest quaver shook her words.

"All right then. I figure you're actually picking Plan B, but we'll pretend it's C. Next step: put the gun down."

She did, placing it near Rex so that he could find it if he woke. Following the Rat's instructions, she set up shade around him and left the last of their water near at hand.

One last kiss, one second to stroke his cheek a final time.

I love you, she thought silently. *I promise I'm coming back for you, once I make sure this bastard can't hurt our kids.*

Heart aching, she straightened, trying to ignore the dark pool of blood that surrounded her Mate.

"Now what?"

"Now, we walk."

As they did, Paige studied him. Freeman was a small man. Scrawny and wiry, not truly strong...she *might* stand a chance in a fight with him....

The Rat must have agreed because he never gave her a chance. He trailed fifty feet behind her, giving orders. Lacking PotBoi52's guidance, he'd come in from the north. And so they trudged, on and on, out into the middle of nothing.

Under the blazing sun, she boiled in her protective jacket and heavy jeans. Freeman sipped from his water bottle but refused to share. As minutes dragged by and sweat poured down her face, Paige found herself growing dizzy.

Bastard. He probably wants me weak with thirst and dehydration. Makes it less likely I can fight back.

By the time the Rat's Jeep came into view, she was staggering.

Freeman, meanwhile, remained cheerful. "There's a box under the driver's seat. Get it and take a seat in the shade."

That was an order she could happily obey. Paige retrieved the box and plunked to the ground.

"There's a pair of handcuffs inside. I want you to cuff your right hand to your left ankle."

Oh hell. If she did that, she'd have no chance to jump the Rat....

Freeman didn't miss that hesitation. "Time to choose, lady. What's it gonna be? Plan B or C?" He took a step back and the muzzle of his rifle rose.

Exhausted, unarmed, and too far away...she chose to delay again. "Plan C," she croaked. Then she clicked the cuffs shut, effectively crippling herself.

One of the Rat's eyebrows rose. "Well, hell. I really took you for a Plan B kinda girl. Glad you're sensible." He tossed her his canteen and backed up. "I need to make arrangements. You catch your breath, stay cool, drink some water. I'll be right back."

Which was kind of a lie: he never really left. Just backed up a hundred feet and made a phone call without taking his eyes off her. Unable to hear anything he said, Paige used the time to catch her breath. No telling when (or if...) an opportunity to escape would arise. She needed to be ready at any moment.

When the Rat returned, he crouched down a few feet away from her. "Everything's settled. All we need to do is pick up the kids—and then I take you to your new home."

'Home'. Oh, that was funny. Paige glared at him and wished looks really could kill.

"One more question." Freeman leaned closer, beady eyes fixed on hers. "Where are the kids?"

For a second, she couldn't even understand what those

words meant. Freeman knew where Rex lived. Why would he ask such an obvious question?

Then the answer hit her, and she began to laugh. Wild, hysterical gales of mockery.

SueSue Mint. Rex's Rat babysitter. She and the children had escaped!

Freeman slid a long, wicked knife from his boot sheath and waved it in front of her eyes. "If you insist, I *will* torture you until you tell me."

"Torture away!" she taunted him. "I don't know where they are. Their sitter took them, and you'll never find them."

"Rat?" His eyes narrowed. "I thought so. That booby-trap in the mud room nearly got me."

Good on you, SueSue, she thought. *You keep my babies safe!*

His nose wrinkled as if he'd bitten a lemon. "Guess it's a good thing I've got you, then."

Like a gut-punch, those words knocked the wind out of Paige. Her throat burned with shame as she realized the truth.

He'd tricked her. A scrawny guy like him couldn't drag her miles through the desert. So, he'd fooled her into walking to his Jeep. *She* had given him the hostage he needed.

All afternoon long, her heart had raced. Bouncing from fear to worry to terror and back. Now, at last, it stilled. As she pondered that awful, disgraceful truth, peace settled over her.

She knew what she had to do now.

Die.

Dead, they couldn't use her against Rex. One shot, one stab, and it would be over. Her family and her love would be safe. All it took was a way to provoke Freeman into a killing rage.

Completely unaware of how the 'game' had changed around him, Freeman kept talking. "This next part will be challenging, but I'm sure you can pull it off. You need to hobble to the back of the Jeep and get in."

Eyes flashing, she raised her chin. "No. I'm not cooperating anymore. Move me yourself, jerk."

His eyes narrowed. "Woman, you do *not* want to pull this shit. Have you ever been tortured?"

"Nope." Damn, she loved her voice right now. Strong, confident, mocking. Lily would be so proud of her 'Omega Wolf.'

"Then let me tell you what's going to happen." Crouching, Freeman tossed that wicked knife back and forth between his hands. "I'll start by peeling your fingernails off, one at a time. If that doesn't make you see sense, I'll take off a couple of fingers."

"Gee, sounds awful!" The Rat's face darkened with fury at her cheerful agreement.

"I don't think you understand…."

No, you're the one that doesn't get it. To cut off my fingers, you need to bring that knife near me. And it's my key to saving Rex.

Wary, sensing a trap, he studied her. And, in the quiet heat of the afternoon, she heard a sound. A dim, rhythmic beat, growing closer.

Thuh-thump. Thuh-thump. Thuh-thump.

Freeman's head snapped up.

A grizzly charged through the desert toward them. Blood soaked its fur and shoulder but that wound didn't even slow it. Eyes blazing with rage, muscles rippling, claws tearing through gravel and dirt, the Bear barreled toward them with shocking speed.

Forgotten, the knife tumbled from the Rat's fingers as he grabbed the rifle slung across his shoulders.

Paige lunged for it too, hooking the strap with her free left hand.

"Let go!" the Rat shrieked, wrenching the gun back and forth, trying to shake her loose.

Paige clung to it like a terrier.

A booted foot lashed out and Paige felt its steel toe slam into her stomach. Air exploded from her lungs. To her horror, she felt the rifle strap slip through her fingers.

"No...."

Triumphant, the Rat spun, shouldering his weapon.

Too late.

Rex plowed into him with the force of a freight train. Bear and Rat flew past her, driven by the power of that charge. A shrill, terrified scream rang out.

And was quickly drowned by an ear-splitting roar.

Then one sharp, terrible 'crack'... and silence.

CHAPTER 19

The room was filled with voices. Low whispers, murmurs. A babbling stream of muttering that slowly washed away the darkness that hid him.

Rex cracked an eye open.

A half-dozen people clustered by the door, conferring. The Donnellys, Aaron King, Bone-Dog, and John Painter, a Bear he knew from Denver.

"Speak of the Devil," said the Wolf. "Someone's come out of hibernation."

Pushing himself up, Rex flexed his bandaged shoulder and was pleased to feel nothing worse than a dull ache. "How's a Bear supposed to sleep with a flock of geese squawking in his bedroom?"

At the sound of his voice, Paige elbowed her way through the crowd and darted to the side of his bed.

The sight of her face, lined with fear and worry, roused his Bear. It grumbled, urging him to nuzzle his Mate and reassure her. He found himself caught, tangled in the marvelous details of her body. The beauty of her round, sweet face. The way that her rebellious bang flipped down across her cheek, begging him to sweep it back. Her touch, her body, her voice…they were magical. In their presence, light filled the world.

He recognized that light now.

Love.

He loved Paige Hall. Loved her, *needed* her so much that no threat would keep him from her side.

Not even the threat of losing her.

Yet, even as he shivered, rocked by those soul-shaking emotions, words escaped him.

"Hey," was all he said.

"Hey yourself." Gently, she settled in beside him, and this time, Rex *did* brush her hair back. "How are you feeling?"

"Fine."

Ah, hell, wasn't he the chatty one… He should say more. Profess his love. Tell her he couldn't live without her. Or, well, at least choke out a couple of sentences.

Fortunately, Paige wasn't as tongue-tied as him. "I'm sorry we woke you."

"Nah, I really am okay." That was better. More than one syllable, anyway. "What happened?"

"Well, you, um, killed Freeman."

"I sure hope so! Be pretty damned disgusted with myself if I couldn't take out one Rat!" When she didn't laugh, Rex winced.

Stupid. She isn't Kin. She doesn't know how savage and violent the Shifter world can be. You've probably scared her half to death.

He scooped up of her slender hands in his big mitts. "Are you okay with that?"

"Yes." Though it was low and quiet, no doubts shook her voice. "By the time you showed up, I was hoping to kill him myself. How *did* you find me, by the way? Freeman and I headed north, not south."

"That Rat made one huge mistake: he threatened you. I

could feel it, even lying there with a bullet in my shoulder. And I knew where to find you. He couldn't have hidden from me if he'd tried."

Finn Donnelly nodded in approval. "Because she's your true Mate. Now in the Rat's defense, only Dragons are supposed to be able to sense when their Mates are in trouble. Not Bears. That's a new thing."

And there it was again. That word.

Mate.

Today, it didn't chill him or summon memories of Ashley's broken body and crushed car. Today, it was a promise, not a threat.

Paige had noticed it too. He could tell by the way she dropped her gaze, by the faint blush that crept delightfully across her cheeks.

"Well, Donnelly, I guess the Hares are right: the world is changing now that magic's back. And I'm glad. Not just because it let me save you, either. It helped me sort things out."

"I don't understand," she whispered, suddenly growing shy.

"When you told me you loved me, I didn't answer. Now I know why. I was running away, just like you said. From the pain of losing Ashley. From the danger of caring about a person so much more fragile than a Bear."

She opened her mouth, probably to defend him against his own accusations. Rex hurried on before she could make him lose his nerve. "When my Bear hauled me out of that coma, raving about you, I realized how wrong I was. You *are* my Mate. You're my heart, the other half of my soul. My Bear knew it from day one. It took a bullet and a kidnapping to drive that fact through *my* thick skull, but I can't deny it any longer. Magic made that impossible."

Normally, blurting out his feelings in front of four guys

would have made him die of shame. Today, Rex didn't give a shit who heard. Proud, he raised his head. "Paige Hall, I love you. I want to marry you, to merge our families into something new and precious. I know what you're thinking." Her eyes, wide and startled as a fawn's, brought a smile to his face. "You're thinking, 'Isn't there supposed to be a question in there someplace?'"

Laughter filled the room, from Donnelly's bass chuckle to his love's silvery giggle. Yet a soft melancholy lingered in Rex's heart. He wasn't out of the woods yet. "I'll get to it, but this is complicated. Paige Hall, would you marry me—even though I can't promise you a safe life? I will do my best. I would die for you, and for our kids. But with these Fangs of Apophis out there... the Shifter world just isn't safe. I can't make promises."

"The only promises I need are wedding vows," she assured him, her face flushed with love and a trust that made his heart sing with joy. Deep inside, his Bear reared onto its hind legs and roared its delight at the sky.

Yet he could not hurry her. This decision would last a lifetime and he wanted that lifetime to be perfect. "Are you sure? You've seen what the Fangs are like. In just the short time we've known each other, both you and your son have been kidnapped."

"And we've been saved. By you."

"But you came here to be safe...."

"I came here because I ran away," she corrected him. "Like you. And I need to stop too. Lily was right. Every day, we can choose to be stronger. Today, I choose to stop running. Today, I choose you, and love."

The last of his objections fell away, leaving nothing but happiness behind. "Then, Paige Hall, will you marry me?"

"I will," she said, eyes bright with tears of joy.

The other guests waded in then, offering congratulations

and claps on the back. Though, Aaron King kept chuckling. "Lily told you that, Miss Hall? It's probably the first time she's ever given someone good advice."

For a time, he simply basked in joy. In the warmth of friendship, the heat of his Mate's love, and passion's whispered promise of a life of ecstasy.

Eventually, however, one nagging worry wiggled its way into his bliss. "Hang on. You never did tell me what happened! After I killed the Rat, I mean."

"Oh, right!" Flushed with happiness, Paige laughed. "Well, you reared back on your hind legs, made this weird gurgling noise, and fainted."

"Okay, okay, I don't need *every* embarrassing detail," he grumbled, to a chorus of chuckles.

"Sorry! Fortunately, we had phone coverage. I called the Donnellys and they came and got you. After that..." Paige waved at the others. "They should tell you. I was busy nursing you and didn't have a lot to do."

King eyed Donnelly, as if daring the Dragon to speak before him. The big man ducked his head instead, and the Wolf took up the story. "The attack on you brought this community together. You probably don't know it because Shifters are an ornery bunch, but you're pretty popular.

"With the information on the Rat's phone, we located two more Fang safehouses. They've been taken out—which should shut down their operations in this area."

"Any sign of that Worm?" The older man shook his head and Rex sighed. "Well that's a good start, but the war isn't won."

"No," the Wolf agreed, "but the Fangs no longer have bases near us. And now that we're onto them, they won't find it so easy to fly under the radar."

"Plus, now we know what they're looking for," Donnelly chimed in.

Like the Dragon was some upstart pup sticking his nose into adult talk, King harried him right back out of the conversation. "I was getting to that. The Sand, Sage, and Big River Packs have agreed to patrol the badlands. Any sign of people driving where they shouldn't, and we'll hunt them down."

Three Packs? That was a hell of a lot of Shifters. "Thank you," he said, with heartfelt relief.

And, of course, the Wolf was in a nipping mood and wouldn't even accept gratitude. "We're not doing it for you. These are our range lands, our territory. We're defending what's ours."

His Bear shuffled and rumbled, annoyed at all that barking.

I know, right? Two weeks ago, they weren't doing shit-all. Now they've got their tails up in the air, proud as hell about defending 'their' land.

His Bear agreed and suggested giving the Wolf a nice swat, just to put him in his place. Tempting as it was, Rex vetoed the idea.

Let's not chase them away before they help. Wolves can be obnoxious but—like Lily—sometimes, you need them.

"Unfortunately, the Rats are as useless as always," King grumbled.

That surprised Rex—since up till now, they were the only Shifter Kind putting full effort into this project. "Oh?"

"They refuse to work with us."

Well, you guys are a snappish bunch and Rats don't care to get bitten.

No point telling King that, though. Rex tried a more tactful approach. "Let me talk to them. I know SueSue pretty well. I bet I can buy info off them." Personally, he doubted the Rats wanted more than a cup of coffee for their spy work, but it let the Wolves save face. "What about that painting Paige and I found?"

King nodded to Donnelly. "Why don't you fill him in?" Rex bit his lip to hide a smile.

The Wolf must not know; otherwise, poor Donnelly wouldn't get a single word in today.

But if the big Dragon was irritated by King's games of dominance, it didn't show. "We still don't know the meaning of the five Shifters. Some of the local Hares are Native and they're going to talk to their tribal Elders and see if anyone knows more. Our best guess is that they're the five people who will summon this monster into the world."

"Nemagorix." Beside him, Paige shivered, and he wrapped an arm around her shoulders.

Standing by her husband, Bree Donnelly nodded. "We don't have much information on that thing or this 'Aegis' he mentioned to you. Further research is necessary."

Disappointing, but not a surprise. "And the painting itself?"

"Torn down," the Hare confessed. "I hate the idea of destroying antiquities, but it was too dangerous. We couldn't find a way to make Nemagorix shut up, so we took his 'phone' away, if you will."

Good. No easy way for the thing to speak to the Fangs, then. It wasn't a perfect solution, but it would do, for now.

"Sounds like you guys have things under control. Not much for me to do except talk to Rats, finish healing…and start planning a wedding," Rex added, smiling at his Mate.

Paige beamed back at him, proud and happy. "And we need to get SueSue a good present. She was a miracle. She spotted Freeman on his way in and got the kids away."

"Did she bring them back," he grumbled, "or do I have to start searching fallout shelters?"

"Yes, she's watching them now. They're out playing around the pool."

His kids were actually in the damn pool—not whining to be taken to Totten Reservoir? Would wonders never cease!

"Huh. I didn't know she liked kids." A speculative gleam lit his eyes. "You think she's interested in a babysitting job?"

"Let's ask her," Paige said, snuggling into the crook of his arms. "Besides, I think the position is opening up!"

* * *

Thank you for reading Damaged Daddy Bear! If you loved it then we are pretty sure you are going to love the next book in the series, Alpha Protector Dragon!

Click here to get Alpha Protector Dragon on Amazon!

Ok, fine…here is a little preview of Alpha Protector Dragon…

CASEY BRIGGS WAITED. HE SAT ON STONE, THE BACKBONE OF Mother Earth, so that she might keep him strong. Dressed in her colors – black shirt, black pants, black tie – he summoned the mantle of her eternal patience, bidding it to settle his agitated heart. Beneath those clothes, hidden to human eyes but not those of the spirits, tattoos covered his arms. Proclaiming his ancestry and his nature in swirling black patterns that would last forever. Or at least as long as his body. Above him, Father Sun burned down, fierce in the desert morning. The shrill cry of a hawk echoed through the still air.

A good omen. The spirits guarded him in this treacherous time.

And so, he waited.

Mirages writhed and twisted at the horizon. From those shimmering lights, a figure emerged. A man, trudging slowly down the remains of an old road. Nearer he came, growing larger, more imposing, with each step.

Casey waited. Today was a momentous day, and the first of its great challenges approached. He would not succumb to eagerness or impatience like some Shifter child.

At last, the stranger stood before him. He was an intimidating man, with short-cropped blonde hair and a scattering of scars. His spirit animal, a great white Dragon, loomed large, its battered maw crisscrossed with scars.

Casey wasn't daunted. His own spirit might be smaller, a lithe black Dragon with the curving horns that marked his Flight. But he knew he was the equal of any Shifter, and today, the spirits blessed him.

The stranger nodded pleasantly. "You must be Casey Briggs, from the Snow Flight."

"Flight of the Snows," he corrected him.

"Right. Finn Donnelly, First Flight."

The arrogance of that name was a slap that couldn't be ignored. "You are from Those Who Have Forgotten Themselves."

Donnelly's expression didn't change – though the icy scales of his Dragon suddenly blazed with a brilliant azure light. Anger. Good. Casey felt a surge of adrenaline as his own Dragon rose to that challenge and unfurled its great wings.

Yet, to give him credit, the white Dragon's words

remained calm. "Is that what you call us? Let's stick to 'First Flight', okay? Little shorter than 'Flight of Those Who Can't Even Remember Why They're Here.'"

"Perhaps, 'The Forgetful Flight'?"

In the Spirit World, two Dragons locked eyes. The white rumbled its disapproval, a deep, bone-shaking growl. The black hissed back, its sinewy tail whipping from side to side. Casey felt its power sing through his blood, calling him to battle.

Until the big man shrugged. "Sure. What the hell. I've been called a lot worse."

The first spark of grudging respect lit in Casey's heart. A humble warrior was a dangerous opponent. One who could not be tricked into a foolish charge.

Calm, he ordered his Dragon. *Let us hear what this outsider wishes to say.*

"Why have you requested this meeting?"

Donnelly gazed out at the vast spread of emptiness that surrounded them. "Before I answer, can I ask one thing? Why did we have to meet at a rock in the middle of nowhere rather than, say, Starbucks?"

And just like that, irritation roiled the calm waters of Casey's soul. "Do you not know this 'rock'?"

The other Dragon scratched his nose. "Is it, uh, granite? Or something like that?"

"This 'rock'," he snapped, "is the Place of Meeting Outsiders. It is here that, in ages past, the Peoples of this land welcomed our Flight. When the Sand, Big River, and Sage Packs sought peace among themselves, they came here, and they bound their Packs by blood and marriage. This is a sacred place! There is no more auspicious site for a meeting!"

"Okay, well, I'm not from around here and I didn't know that," said the Forgetful idiot. "Look, I'm not trying to talk smack about your rock. I'm just saying that it's hot and I could really go for an iced latte right now. And Starbucks' seats are more comfortable," he added, as he swept a rock out from under himself.

How typical! Everything came down to indulgence and luxury for Those Who Have Forgotten Themselves. Were they even Dragons any longer – or just big, greedy lizards? "Again, I ask you," Casey said through gritted teeth, "why did you wish to speak to me?"

"Because my Flight has forgotten something," the big man said with a wide, guileless smile. One that made it hard to hold a grudge – even for a member of the proud Flight of the Snows. "We're hoping you guys still remember it. You were at Fairburn's meeting, right?"

Rex Fairburn. Casey's lip twitched with disgust. The resorts that Bear built devoured the land and the silence with a hunger greater than any fallen Dragon's. When Fairburn put out a call, asking all the Shifters of the Southwest to come hear of a new 'danger', Miles Kennedy, the Alpha of the Flight of the Snows, ignored him. "He is a destroyer of tradition," he told his brothers of the Flight. "What threatens him does not threaten us."

Despite that, Casey *had* gone. The Bear was as blind and stupid as they come, yet no one could accuse him of failing his duties. He protected his people and his town with honor. That duty, that faithfulness, earned him the right of a hearing.

And what a hearing it was! The words spoken still burned their way through Casey's dreams. Oh, not Fairburn's worries about some new enemies, the 'Fangs of Apophis'. The Dragon neither knew nor cared about them. New enemies, old enemies… it was all the same. Those who remained vigilant didn't need to worry.

No, let the other Shifters fret about these Fangs. What

had shaken Casey to the bottom of his soul was Finn Donnelly's announcement.

Wellsprings had returned. Founts of magic, they faded in ages past, leaving the world dull and mundane. Abandoning their protectors, the Dragons, to empty, meaningless existence. Now, the Wellsprings woke. Once more, Dragons were summoned to their most ancient duty: to protect the sacred waters that breathed life and wonder into the world. With magic's return, the Rite of Claiming was reborn. No longer would his Kind drift through the ages, alone. Fate's web grew strong again. Its touch, subtle and eternal, drew Dragons to their true Mates.

CONTINUE THE NEXT STORY IN THE SHIFTERS OF THE AEGIS series, Alpha Protector Dragon, here on Amazon...